Lock Down Publications and Ca$h Presents

A Thug's Street Princess

By
Meesha

First Edition 2024

Printed in the United States of America

This is a work of fiction. Names, characters, places, and incidents either are products of the author's imagination or are used fictitiously. Any similarity to actual events or locales or persons, living or dead, is entirely coincidental.

Lock Down Publications
P.O. Box 944
Stockbridge, GA 30281
www.lockdownpublications.com

Like our page on Facebook: Lock Down Publications
www.facebook.com/lockdownpublications.ldp

Stay Connected with Us!

Text **LOCKDOWN** to 22828 to stay up-to-date with new releases, sneak peaks, contests and more…

Like our page on Facebook:
Lock Down Publications

Join Lock Down Publications/The New Era Reading Group

Visit our website:
www.lockdownpublications.com

Follow us on Instagram:
Lock Down Publications

Email Us: We want to hear from you!

Chapter 1

Honey

"Honey! Bitch, Savannah out there about to get her ass whooped. You better go save her."

Glancing up from my bunk, I frowned at Sunshine because she was out of her mind coming to me about the bullshit. Not only did she come in my cell, but her big, black ass didn't even knock.

"First of all, don't ever walk in my shit disrespectfully. You wait until you're invited in this muthafucka. The only folks that can enter unannounced is the funky ass pigs! Secondly, I don't give a fuck about Savannah. I've told her time and time again about her mouth. It has fallen on deaf ears. I'm done trying to protect anybody in this raggedy muthafucka. Get out!"

Watching Sunshine leave with her tail tucked between her legs, I felt bad about not going out to the yard to help Savannah. Saving folks was a thing of the past for me. Nobody knew my days as an inmate were basically over and I wasn't trying to fuck it up by fighting a battle that wasn't mine. Twenty-four hours was all I had left. Then the kid would be free to a certain extent, but I would no longer have to accept anybody telling me when to eat, shit, or sleep.

See, when I first entered the custody of law enforcement, they booked my ass into Cook County jail in Chicago for a year. After the judge found me guilty of possession and intent to distribute heroin, they shipped me straight to the maximum-security prison where I'd been for the past eight years. Hell, anywhere was better than the deplorable conditions I had to suffer through in the County. That muthafucka needed to be burned to the ground in my opinion.

Before Sunshine invaded my thoughts, I was reminiscing about the reason behind my incarceration. I would have never imagined spending years behind bars but that was the price to pay for the dumb shit I'd done. There was no use crying over spilled milk because my bid was coming to an end. Closing my eyes as I relaxed on my bunk, my mind went back to the day I got knocked.

Rockin' to Meek Mills' "Dreams and Nightmares" as I rolled down Chicago Avenue, heading to my girl Monae's house. My phone rang and my man Cheese's name popped up on the dash. I hit the button to answer the phone with a quickness.

"Yeah, babe?" I asked while turning the music down.

"I know you didn't take my car!" he yelled in my ear.

"Damn, since when did driving your car become a problem?"

"When I have two birds in that muthafucka, Honey! I was coming right back to drop that shit off, yo!"

"Calm down, shit! I can make the fuckin' drop for you. It's not like I'm not part of your team, so stop hollering at me like I'm your child. Shoot me the addy and I'll take care of it."

I was so mad at his tone that I sped right through a red fuckin' light. Before I knew it, there were blue and red lights on my ass. I started sweating bullets as I pulled to the right side of the street.

"Cheese, I-I'm being pulled over," I stammered.

"Fuck, Honey! Why did you take the fuckin' car? You know them muthafuckas are always fuckin' with a nigga whenever I'm driving. Dammit, man! They gon' search the car, baby. You gon' have to eat this shit. Don't tell them

A THUG'S STREET PRINCESS | MEESHA

*muthafuckas shit! I promise, I got you. It's your first offense
and you will get the bare minimum sentence. I'm gon' ride
this shit out with you."*

Before I could respond to what Cheese said, I peeped the
officer walking up to the car with his hand on his gun. I
immediately hit the end button on the steering wheel and
waited to find out my fate. After all was said and done, the
car was searched, I was cuffed and put in the back of the
squad car. The ride to the station was silent but my mind was
going a mile a minute.

At the police station, I was led to one of the interrogation
rooms and cuffed to a chair. I sat in the cold room for about
thirty minutes before anyone even came in to check on me. A
detective entered with a manila file in his hand, and I knew
right away, the bullshit was about to begin. I was badgered
for two hours by a couple of detectives that wanted me to
give Cheese up for a lesser sentence. When I wouldn't budge,
they threatened to throw the book at my ass, but I stuck to
the story of the drugs being mine.

I took that hit like a champ; all for the love I had for
Cheese. At the age of seventeen he came into my life at a
time when I didn't have anyone else. My father had left my
mother when I was very young, and I hadn't heard from him
again. Life was good when it was just me and my mother. It
wasn't until I was about thirteen that things started to change.
All the time we spent together when she was off work
became time for her and the man my mother finally allowed
into her life.

James was pretty cool at first, and I liked him. We would
do many things as a family and James treated me like the
father I'd always wanted. When I turned fifteen, I started
peeping how he would watch me whenever I walked through
our apartment. The way he licked his lips as his eyes roamed
my body made me uncomfortable. I didn't say anything to
my mother because I didn't want to jump to conclusions
because James hadn't said nor done anything inappropriately

other than staring at me lustfully. At the time, I started developing at a rapid pace. My breasts were growing, and my ass was getting a lot bigger. I no longer looked like a young child, but I was maturing into a young woman.

As the months went on, I took matters into my own hands and made sure I stayed fully clothed when home, even when my mother was present. I didn't want to give James any reason to say I was enticing him sexually in any way. It didn't matter what I had on, he gawked at me at every turn. Finally fed up with his perverse demeanor, I decided to tell my mother about my concerns. I called her into my bedroom so we would be out of earshot of James. Once I told her what her man was doing, she immediately called me a liar while screaming in my face. What I thought would be a private conversation between us turned into James standing in the doorway of my bedroom, swearing he never looked at me in a sexual manner.

James kept his distance after that, but his lustful glares continued. It wasn't until two years later that he finally made his move. My mother left for work at her overnight job, and I was minding my business in my room. I had installed a knob on my door that had a lock so I would feel safe being in the house with James. While watching *Love & Hip Hop Atlanta,* I could hear James trying to break into my room. My heart started beating in my chest at a rapid pace as I jumped out of bed and ran across the small room. Before I could brace my body against the door it came flying open.

I backed away from James because he was gripping his penis as he stared at me. I had on a pair of pajama shorts that ended right under my ass, a tank to match, and a pair of black socks.

James didn't say a word as he walked further into my room. He took a wide step, grabbed me by the arm, and pulled me into his body with force. He tried to kiss me, and I fought him off with all my might by punching him in his chest then biting his arm. James smacked me hard as hell, drawing blood from lip but found a way to grope my breast. I was stunned momentarily but shook that shit off. When I went to scream, he covered my mouth with his hand, and I bit his pinky finger until he drew back. I then kicked him in his balls, causing him to double over. I hauled ass out of the apartment and ran down the wintery streets of Chicago.

Cheese and some of his boys were coming out of the gas station when I ran up to them crying for help. With no questions asked, Cheese allowed me to get in his truck and slammed the door. James rounded the corner, looking around frantically I lowered the window informing Cheese that the man in the black shirt tried to rape me. James approached the truck and I damn near pissed on myself. But he was pointed in the wrong direction; purposely.

When James ran into the alley, Cheese and his boys followed behind him. A few minutes passed then shots rang out. Everybody except James exited the alley quickly. Cheese jumped in his truck and pulled off. He asked where I lived and dropped me off in front of my house. Before he let me out, he asked for my number, but I didn't have one to give him. My mama always said if I wanted a phone, I would have to buy it myself. But she wouldn't let me work. What a joke. Instead, he scribbled his on a napkin and told me to hit him up if needed.

I knew Cheese had killed James but I was smart enough to know not to utter a vowel about what transpired. The code of the streets was, if you saw something, you kept your fuckin' mouth shut. Plus, Cheese pulled his gun and used it for me. There was no way I would say anything. That night, I showered and threw my pajamas in a dumpster down the street from my home before climbing into bed to get some sleep.

My mother came home to find out James was not there. Victoria Love barged into my bedroom, asking me about his whereabouts. Every time I told her I hadn't seen James, she called me a liar and accused me of making him leave because he couldn't handle my accusations. I'd told her the honest to God truth about how I felt about James and she didn't believe me back then, so there was no way I was going to tell her what had taken place the night before. She couldn't make me know where he was so I just kept repeating that I hadn't seen him. Needless to say, because my mother's perverted man "left her" she put her only child out with the clothes on her back.

Being seventeen years old with nowhere to go, I was scared as hell. Walking down the street in the dead of winter with no coat, a pair of jogging pants, a t-shirt, and fuzzy socks, I walked aimlessly. As I turned the corner by the very gas station I'd run to the night before, there were police everywhere. At that moment, the coroner van pulled up and I knew James had been found. I did an about face into someone's chest.

Cheese stared down at me with a scowl on his face. "What are you doing out here without a coat?" he asked.

"My mama put me out. I don't have anywhere to go."

"I told you to hit me up, Shawty. I should go peel her muthafuckin' skull back. She gon' regret doing you like that when the truth comes out about that nigga. Come on."

Cheese took me to his house and had been looking out for me ever since. He didn't let me know what he did for a living until after I graduated high school. On my graduation day, I also turned eighteen years old. Cheese bought me a Mercedes Benz truck, after countless hours of teaching me how to drive, and took me on a shopping spree. That was the moment I discovered how old he was and why he never tried to sleep with me. Cheese was twenty-five years old and once I was considered an adult, he turned my ass out. We fucked every which way but loose and I loved it. I started cooking his dope, counting his money, balancing his books, and I'd popped a few opps for him, too. I was Bonnie and he was Clyde of the hood. The bitches were big mad because a young bitch, as they would say, captured the heart of a nigga they could only fuck and suck.

Damn near every day I was fighting bitches behind Cheese. He always came back with the same explanation; they were jealous of what we had together. Being the naïve girl I was, I believed that shit. We were happy and I did everything possible to prove I was down for him. Then I got popped.

Cheese held me down the entire time I was on lock at the County. He put money on my books, bought commissary, sent me all the latest releases from the dope authors of Lock Down Publications, and never missed a visit. When I was shipped to the women's prison in Seattle, Washington, Cheese never showed up, but he kept in touch via letters and emails. He also continued to make sure I was straight. That only lasted for the first six months of my arrival. After that, he was as silent as a lamb.

For eight years I rode out my sentence with only the backing of my homegirl Charlie and my cousin Cheno. When Charlie was released three years into my bid, Cheno took her under his belt. My girl been holding shit down for the both of us. The two of them were the only people that knew I was getting out the next day. The less folks who knew, the better. Cheese would have to see me once I touched down.

***

I was anxious to get the fuck out of the place I'd called home for the past eight years, so I was up bright and early after barely sleeping the night before. To pass time, the last of my commissary was divided so I could distribute everything between my girls. I was due to be released at ten o'clock and it was eight-thirty. Time was moving faster than it ever had behind these walls and I was grateful for it.

"Honey, can I come in?" Savannah's voice softly came through the metal door of my cell. I really didn't want to deal with her troublesome ass, but I was curious to find out what she had to say.

"Yeah, come on in," I said, never looking up from the task I was trying to complete. The door closed and Savannah walked over to me as I took items out of my cabinet. "What can I do for you?"

"Sunshine told me you basically said fuck me yesterday. I needed you, Honey, and you left me out there to fend for myself." Savannah's voice sounded so sad, but I didn't feed into that shit. In fact, her attempt at guilt tripping me only pissed me off.

I had been fighting Savannah's battles since the day she walked into the facility. That was damn near five years ago. Savannah would talk shit to everybody because she knew I wouldn't allow anybody to fuck with her. I was her bodyguard when I should've been teaching her how to protect herself. Glancing over my shoulder, I stared at the black eye she tried to hide. Savannah's arm was in a cast, and she had four stitches along her right temple. Whoever fucked her up, kicked her ass good.

"What you do this time, Savannah?" I asked but I truly didn't give a fuck, to be honest.

"No, I'm asking the questions!" she screamed.

Chuckling lowly, I bit my bottom lip because baby girl almost got the piss slapped out of her. She got lucky though because I was hours away from walking out of there. "I'm listening. Speak on that shit, Savannah. Don't get carried away because I can only check myself once a day. You got a pass a few seconds ago. I don't think I'll be able to contain myself a second time."

"Why you didn't have my back? I could've been killed out there and you didn't even bother to show your face!" She yelled, poking me in the chest with her finger.

11

I grabbed that muthafucka and bent it at an odd angle, then I clutched her neck before pushing my thumb into her throat tightly. "Bitch, if you ever put your hands on me again, I'll kill yo' bitch ass." I said pushing her away from me. "I've told you too many times to leave these muthafuckas alone. You didn't listen and that's on you. I won't always be around to save yo' ass because you want to run yo' pussy licka. Yo' mouth gon' get you killed in here, Savannah."

"I didn't initiate that shit yesterday! Day—"

"Savannah! I don't give a fuck what happened! The shit had nothing to do with me! You got yo'self in that predicament and you had to get yo'self out. From the looks of it, you only added fuel to the fire. Get ready to get beat the fuck up from this day forth." There was a slight knock on my door, and I groaned loudly walking away from Savannah. "Come the fuck in!"

"Ayeeeeee, what it do, sis? Y'all having a party?" Santa asked stepping into the small cell with Sunshine, Marcia, and Yvonne behind her. At least I didn't have to go find them bitches individually to give them the shit I had sorted.

"It's too early for y'all to be in here making all that damn noise. Why are y'all here anyway?" I asked.

"We heard you were about to beat the shit out of Vannah and you know we don't do that around here. We're sisters, Honey. I suggested we come in and defuse the situation before it got out of hand. The last thing you want is to end up back in the hole."

Yvonne had a point and none of that had entered my mind. My release would've been prolonged for months behind me whooping Savannah's ass. I stared at Savannah and felt sorry for her. She wasn't going to make it without me.

Opening my arms to her, she walked into them and held me tight. "I'm sorry for putting my hands on you like that, knowing you weren't a threat to me. You need to go a couple rounds with these hoes to get your fight game up," I said motioning to the other girls. "If you don't, you're gon' be eating knuckle sandwiches for breakfast, lunch, and dinner."

"Why would I have to do that when I have you for back up?"

I took a deep breath because I knew the time had come for me to tell them what was going on. I looked at all of my girls and took a step away from the circle. I didn't know how they were going to react for not telling them I was being released, but there was no way around the truth.

"That's where you're wrong. You won't have me around to protect you. I won't be around at all to be honest. I'll be getting out in a matter of hours, actually." Reaching over to the items on the desk, I picked up one of the piles and handed it to Savannah. "This is my leftover commissary. I won't be needing any of it after today."

The look of sadness was on all of their faces and I felt myself getting very emotional. For years we rolled together, and we knew the day would come for all of us to go our separate ways. I'd known for months when I would be released. I couldn't tell them because if word got out, someone may have tried to do any little thing to get me in trouble. That was the reason I spent a few weeks in the hole voluntarily.

"Congratulations, Honey." Yvonne said hugging me. "I already know why you kept that shit on the low. There are no hard feelings, sis. Don't forget a bitch once you get outta here. Do something with your life; I don't want to see you back in here."

"Thanks, Yvonne. I'm gon' miss all of y'all," I said looking around the cell.

Savannah threw the items I gave her at my feet and walked out. What was I supposed to do, chase her? Nah, Honey didn't play those type of games. So, I allowed her to leave without another word. Sunshine and the others wasted no time getting their items and Savannah's. As we chopped it up while I finished getting my things together, I gave them basically everything except my journals. All the rest of that shit went to the trash. Time flew by and before I knew it, it was time for me to blow that joint.

"Love, it's time to go," the CO yelled into the cell. "You got five minutes. Anything after that, yo' ass staying in here another year."

"Shid, you got me fucked up. Give me two minutes to say goodbye to my people then I'll be honored for you to walk me out of this dirty ass place."

The CO stood outside the door and I loved on my girls for the last time. If I could, I'd take all of them with me, but that wasn't the way the system worked. They had to do the time for the crime they committed. Just like I had to do. I was going to look after them until they too were released. The tears that ran down my face were both happy and sad tears, and I swear it would be the last muthafuckin time I'd shed another.

Chapter 2

Honey
Ten months later
"Honey, you have a call in the office!"

Lewis, the head mechanic, called out as I was putting the final bolts back in place on the tire of the Mercedes truck I was working on. All the studying and experience I'd put in while in prison paid off for me once I got out. When I was released, the joy of going back to Chicago was short lived because the muthafuckas threw a monkey wrench into my plans. I wasn't told I had to spend a year in a halfway house until I collected all my belongings at the desk. Saying a bitch was mad was an understatement. I wanted to tear the warden's head clean off. I didn't trip because going home was my top priority. If I had to sit under the state's rules for another year, so be it. I'd rather do that shit and be off papers completely than having to check in every week with a curfew. At least I'd be able to move freely and get fresh air every day.

"Hello," I said as I cradled the receiver on my ear with my shoulder while wiping the oil from my hands.

"Hi, Honey, it's Kylie. I have some news for you."

"What's going on?"

"In one week, I'll be coming by to pick you up."

"Pick me up for what?" I asked with an attitude.

I knew damn well they weren't about to tell me some shady shit so close to me being completely free. Two months meant a lot to someone who had been locked away from the world for the past nine plus years. Even though I had been back into the real world working and meeting new people, it was nothing like going back home to the streets of Chicago.

"No need to get upset. I promise the news I have will make you smile from ear to ear. Anyway, back to what I was saying. I have a one-way ticket to Chicago for you. I'm picking you up Monday to escort you to the airport. You will officially be off probation to live life any way you want."

"You lying!" I screamed, fighting back the tears that stung my eyes. A couple of my coworkers came rushing to the office along with my boss. I waved them off, wiping the tears away with a faint smile as I tuned back in to what Kylie was saying.

"Nope. I wouldn't play with you like that. It's true, Honey. You are free!"

"Thank you so much, Kylie, for all you have done for me."

The day I met Kylie, she accompanied me to the halfway house I was placed in after my release. Drama met me at the door the minute I stepped over the threshold. The bitches had rules and regulations that I wasn't cool with following. Dana, the woman in charge, didn't oversee shit because she was afraid of the tenants. They controlled her ass but wasn't going to control me. I had to show them I couldn't be bullied and that was some shit they learned the hard way.

Kylie rode my nerves like a hoe on a dick because she was constantly called to the house. If muthafuckas learned to leave me alone there wouldn't have been any problems. Until then, I was fighting like Laila Ali every day. Kylie sat me down after I busted the ringleader's head, sending her to the hospital to get sixteen stitches. Asking what I liked to do with my life, she somehow got me a job at the Mercedes Benz dealership as a mechanic. To be honest, Kylie saved my life. If it wasn't for her, I would've been right back in prison to finish out my sentence. Kylie made the incident go away and I didn't ask how she did it. She went against all the rules and regulations by going out of her way to make sure I was always straight.

"Are you still there?" Kylie asked.

"Yeah, I didn't think this day would ever come. I'm two months shy of when I was told I'd get out and I just wasn't expecting this."

"Well, get ready, girlfriend! Chitown isn't going to be ready for the new and improved Honey Love!"

I laughed hard as hell because Kylie wanted to be black so bad. Being a white girl, she always tried to talk like she was about that life whenever she was around me. I let her be great so her ego wasn't bruised. All I could tell her was not to talk that shit to anyone else. It would fuck me up if she got her ass whooped, thinking every black person would allow that shit.

"Chicago was never ready for me. I'm not the same eighteen-year-old who got caught being dumb. Believe me, the city will be safe. I owe you, man."

"You don't owe me anything. When I see the good in someone, I will make sure they strive in everything they set out to do. And, Honey, that someone is you. I've always said if I met a person who I truly believed in, they would want for nothing, as long as they stayed out of trouble and go out there and make something of themselves. Everything I've done for you was all in God's plan. All I ask is for you to pay it forward when the time is right."

"Soon as I get on my feet, I'll look into doing just that."

"Okay, well I'll see you Sunday. We're going to hit up the malls. I can't send you back home looking like what you've been through, now can I?" Kylie asked with a chuckle.

"I hear you and I appreciate that. You've done enough, White Chocolate. I'll cover myself this time around."

"Get off my phone, Honey. Stay out of trouble. You're almost at the finish line."

Kylie ended the call and I jumped for joy before returning to work. The rest of my shift went by without a hitch. When it was time for me to clock out, I had a quick sit-down with Mr. Christopher. He told me how proud he was of me and he was going to miss having me on his team. He was the one who trained me the first two weeks I was on the job. Even though I learned the majority of the techniques in prison, there was always room for me to learn more.

"Honey, I've been waiting for the day you get out from under the system. You are a little rough around the edges, but that's to be expected with all you've been through. With that being said, I will have a package ready for you before you leave. You earned everything you've accomplished. Please stay out of trouble and do right with your life. If you need me in any way, I'm a phone call away."

"Thank you, Mr. Christopher. I appreciate you giving me a chance with my background. I have plenty of experience under my belt and it's only up from here. It won't be long before I open my own shop. I just have a little more saving to do and I'll be alright."

"That's what I like to hear. Your determination is through the roof, and I have faith that you will accomplish your goals legally."

I sat back and smirked at his ass. Just because I was in prison didn't mean I was guilty of the crime. That was part of loving a muthafucka more than they loved you. I knew for a fact; it would never happen again and was a true lesson learned.

"No doubt. Look, thanks again and I'll see you tomorrow. I have to get to this damn house before they try to say I was out trickin' off or some shit."

"Take the week off, Honey. Get yourself together for the big payback." I looked at him crazy because I'd just told him I was trying to stack my paper. Why would I be willing to take time off knowing I had no way of making that money back? "I know what you're thinking, and you have nothing to worry about. I will make sure you get compensated for that time."

"I'm gon' hold you to that. I'll call you the day before I'm set to leave so I can pick up that package."

Mr. Christopher nodded as I left his office. I cleaned everything out of my locker and said goodbye to my coworkers before making my way to the bus stop. It was the beginning of summer and the air was comfortable but warm. I took off my work shirt to allow the breeze to grace my skin. At twenty-eight years old, I'd come a long way from being the young girl with B cup titties, a pudgy stomach, and a semi-flat ass. Now, I was a 36 C, with wide hips, washboard abs, and an ass that was round and fluffy.

I wore baggy clothes every day because I didn't go out to enjoy myself. The only time I was outside of the halfway house was to go to work. All that shit was going to change once I got back to Chicago. I felt like a born-again virgin. Ten years was a long time for anybody to go without sex. I learned sex was a want, not a need. It wasn't hard but mentally I had to train myself to be out of sight, out of mind when it came to that shit.

As I stood at the bus stop, the sun was beaming and I was glad when the bus pulled in front of me. Climbing on, I paid my fare while speaking to the driver then made my way to the back. I was relieved that there weren't many people onboard because I hated occupying a seat next to others. There was a nigga sitting back with his eyes locked on my physique as he watched my every move. Soon as I was within his reach, he had the nerve to grab my arm.

"Damn, sexy, what's yo' name?"

"Get the fuck out my face." I snarled, snatching away without losing stride.

One thing I hated was a muthafucka invading my personal space. It didn't take touching me to ask a question. I sat down, realizing he was talking mad shit. I tried my best to ignore his ignorance, but I couldn't hold my tongue any longer once he disrespected me directly.

"Bitch, I didn't want yo' manly lookin' ass anyway. I was trying to put a smile on yo' mean ass face."

This muthafucka had the nerve to name-call somebody when he looked like an older version of Kodak Black. His hair appeared as if he hadn't washed it since his high school days. The clothes he wore had seen better days; in the late nineties. Not to mention, the nigga was shaped like a loaded potato. But he was trying to clown my ass.

Standing at five feet, five inches, I was born with skin the color of caramel, natural hair that I wore in a ponytail, and my body was fit. Of course, he wouldn't know that because of the oil-stained clothes I wore. His ass wasn't expecting me to say anything in return, but he was sadly mistaken. My stint in the prison systems taught me to never allow anyone to play in your face. No matter who the fuck they were.

"Did I ask yo' uglass to help with anything? Let me find out you jealous because the muscles in my arms put yo' flab to shame. Or could it be that keg you luggin' around and I'm sportin' a six pack? I'm really trying to figure out why you so pressed because I didn't turn into putty when you spit that weak ass line to me. I mean, you have a face only a mother could love, nigga."

A dude sitting across the aisle laughed out loud. Sloppy Joe's face balled up in anger because clearly, he was embarrassed by what I'd said. I meant every word and didn't give a damn how he felt about it. All he had to do was take the rejection and shut up. Not him though. He jumped to his feet, charging me with his fists balled at his sides. As I snatched my mace off my belt clip, his ass was laid out in the aisle on his back.

"Nigga, don't ever attempt to put yo' hands on a female in my presence. You muthafuckas need to understand when yo' advances fall flat!" The dude who laughed was standing over Sloppy Joe and it looked as if he was wishing he'd get up.

My stop was approaching so I pulled the chord to let the driver know to stop. I stepped around my savior and lowly thanked him. When the bus came to a halt, I hurried off without looking back. Whatever took place after that, I wanted no parts of. The incident was just the beginning of the bullshit.

Soon as I entered the house, the loudmouth named Danielle came waltzing out of the kitchen with a banana in hand. Being me, I didn't acknowledge the mug she threw my way and continued on to the room. The bitch followed and I breathed deeply because Danielle was nitpicking and had no clue what I'd endured on my journey home. When I kept bumping heads with the females in the house, Kylie pulled a few strings to get me a single person room. Seeming I was a little bit older than the others; it made a lot of sense not to share space with anyone else.

There were plenty of mutters that could be heard around me about how I was given special treatment. What they didn't know was it was in their best interest to keep me out of their company. In other words, they were being saved from the bitch I'd turned into throughout the years. I walked over the threshold and closed the door behind me. When the sound of the knob hitting the wall alerted me, I automatically turned around to see what transpired.

"Are you out of your mind? Don't ever close a door in my face!" Danielle screamed.

Tossing my bag on the bed, I ignored the hell out of her. Being so close to getting out of the house Kylie's words echoed in my head. *Stay out of trouble, Honey.* I also briefly thought about the day Danielle had to be rushed to the hospital to get her head sewn back together. One would think she would just leave me the fuck alone. That was too much like right for Danielle though. Knowing the situation could turn ugly I opted to act as if she wasn't even there. My actions only infuriated Danielle more, but she was already set to go before I even arrived.

"I know you hear me talking to your dirty ass!"

"Hey, Danni, go find somebody else to play with. I'm too grown to put up with yo' bullshit today."

"*I'm too grown to put up with yo' bullshit,*" she mimicked in a childish voice causing me to chuckle. "Bitch, do I look like a joke to you?"

"Actually, yes. My question to you is, why you want to fuck with me? The last ass whoopin' I put on yo' ass wasn't enough, huh? You working on the finale, I see."

Danielle held an evil grin on her face as she backed away from the door. She must've thought about the assault I mentioned and thought twice about coming for me. I, in turn, slammed the door and toed off my work boots. The only thing I wanted to do was take a shower then go to sleep. My mind was on being freed from the invincible shackles I'd been confined to for so long. All that other bullshit Danielle could keep for the next parolee who entered the house after me. I knew Danielle had plans to attack, I just didn't know when it would take place. When it presented itself, I would have to defend myself like the lioness I was.

Gathering everything I would need to take with me to the bathroom, I eased my feet into my Nike slides and walked across the small room. As I reached for the knob, I could hear hushed murmurs coming from the other side of the door. Shaking my head, I listened closely.

"We gon' catch her when she comes out. Honey goes to the shower almost the same time every night. No mercy. Y'all hear me? When one swing, we all swing or whoever doesn't will be getting fucked up next. We are beating her ass before she leaves this house."

"Wait, she's leaving? When?"

"It doesn't matter, Sarah. You worried about the wrong shit." Danielle sneered. "Focus on stomping this hoe."

"Danielle, get away from that door!" Dana yelled. "I will call your probation officer if there's any trouble in this house tonight."

I took that opportunity to leave the room. Danielle and her minions were at the far end of the hall looking like they were ready to attack. I wasn't worried because all it would take was for me to work her ass over first. Danielle probably had three inches on me and she was heavier than I was. She was a very beautiful girl who would have no problem getting a man, but her attitude was the thing that made her so ugly. I had the advantage over her because I was a trained boxer and was far from scary. She was only tough when she had folks to help her fight. I stood alone at all times.

Entering the bathroom, I made sure to lock up behind me. I didn't waste any time disrobing then turned the shower on to the hottest temperature. The bathroom was still clean from when I cleaned it before heading to work that morning. If it wasn't for me, it would be nasty as hell because no one cared about keeping anything disinfected around the house. I brushed my teeth and stepped into the tub. The water pounded all my stress away and relaxed my muscles. I washed a few times and got out. After moisturizing my body, I slipped on a pair of black lounge pants and a sports bra of the same color. I made sure to get all of my toiletries and left the bathroom.

I stepped into the hall and was met by a punch to the face. Everything I held in my hands fell to the floor and I swung in return. Sarah's little scrawny ass hit the wall, alerting Dana to run into the hall. It was three bitches on me trying their best to beat me into a coma, but that shit was wishful thinking on their part. I wasn't going down without a fight.

"Stop it now!" Dana screamed as she threw bodies away from the commotion. "Tanisha, come help me!"

It sounded like a herd of elephants running down the stairs as the other girls in the house came to assist breaking up the fight. I grabbed Danielle by the knotless braids she had in her head and rocked her ass to sleep. The pent-up anger I had inside was being released on her face. She swung wildly, never hitting me in the process. Wrapping the braids around my hand, I made it impossible for her to get more than an inch away from my fist.

"Honey, please let her go!" Dana pleaded.

Feeling something wet on my hand, I focused on Danni, realizing I had her ass leaking. Throwing a few more haymakers while listening to her howl every time she tried to break loose, my hand was finally pried away and I was guided back to my room by Tanisha. Another girl by the name of Sasha entered with all of my belongings. Inspecting the damage I'd done to my knuckles, I sat at my desk and got out the first aid kit I kept in the drawer.

"You've been avoiding Danni all this time and you want to allow her to taunt you now, Honey? You have a week before you are out of here!"

"Tanisha, those bitches didn't taunt me! They plotted on my ass and got dealt with. That was self-defense at its best and I'm standing on that shit!" I snapped. "I was minding my own business and they came fuckin' with me. What was I supposed to do, huh? The same shit y'all do when Danni approaches y'all? Never in a day. I will forever stand up for myself and deal with the consequences and repercussions when they come to me. I bet that bitch tread lightly around me while I'm still in this raggedy ass house."

Bandaging the cuts on my right hand, Tanisha's words played back in my mental. Not only did Danielle know I was getting out, but so did she and I wanted to know how everybody knew when I'd just found out myself. I threw the bloody alcohol wipes in the trash and stood in front of Tanisha.

"How does everybody know when the fuck I'm leaving this muthafucka?"

"Well, Kylie called Dana and she had the phone on speaker while she sat in the living room watching Wheel of

Fortune. I was in the kitchen making a sandwich, and Danielle was sitting at the table on the laptop."

"Hmmm. That explains it. Well, thank y'all for not letting me beat here ass worse than I did. I may be going back to prison for the next two months instead of being free. I'll find out in the morning. Until then, I'm going to bed. See your way out and turn off that light."

Chapter 3

Honey

Kylie was at the house bright and early the next morning waking me from my sleep. She had papers in hand stating I could go to a hotel until I boarded the plane the following Monday. As I packed my duffle bag with the little bit of clothing I owned, Danielle was being escorted out by the police.

"Bitch, I'm gon' catch yo' ass soon as I do this hot year. Watch yo' muthafuckin' back, Honey!"

I couldn't do anything but laugh because she was a whole clown. Danni would forever get the ass end of the stick fucking with me. Kylie was forever coming through and I was appreciative as hell. Throwing the strap over my shoulder, I glanced around the room and didn't care about all the shit I was leaving behind. I'd been working just as long as I'd been in the halfway house and still had all of the money in my account. It was nothing for me to hit the stores and get right.

"I'm ready," I said walking toward the door.

"You leaving everything else behind?"

"Yeah. It's mainly work wear and stuff I had when I first got locked up. I don't need any of that shit. When we go to the mall, I'll just have to get a large luggage to put everything in. It's not a big deal. I'll be straight."

"Alright, let's go, then."

I left the house and didn't say goodbye to anyone. Leave the past in the past, right? That was exactly what I planned to do. Kylie hit the locks on her car from her key fob. I stood admiring the Beamer and it reminded me of the life Cheese used to live back in the day. Being able to drive expensive cars and get whatever I wanted was something I loved. But at the same time, I was going to make it my business to come up legally.

"This is a nice car, Kylie," I said sitting in the passenger seat. "I know damn well you're not making money like that being a damn parole officer."

She laughed shifting the gear in reverse then backed out of the driveway. "You're absolutely correct. I'm a silver spoon baby. My father was the owner of several banks before he died. I didn't want any parts of the business. My brothers are running the show on that end. He left me with a substantial nest egg that will hold me over for the rest of my life. I only work because I want to do things that will help people get their lives on track."

Changing lanes, Kylie seemed like she was lost in her thoughts for a second. She tapped her fingers on the steering wheel as she drove in the direction of the Westfield shopping center. Turning in my direction briefly, Kylie paid attention to the road.

"Honey, let me ask you something."

"I'm listening," I said giving her my undivided attention.

"Correct me if I'm wrong, but you didn't commit the crime you served time for, did you?"

"I was caught with the drugs, Kylie. Guilty as charged, mamas." I said without hesitation.

"LaDarrius 'Cheese' Hawkins is mentioned in your transcripts as being your boyfriend at the time. I know you took the fall for him, Honey. I love you like a sister and want you to stay far away from him when you get back to Chicago. I never want to see your name come through the system again. Okay?"

"You have nothing to worry about when it comes to me and Cheese. I'm not going to lie; I was dating him at the time of my incarceration, but the charges were all mine. He showed me how deep his love for me was when he didn't show his face at visitation throughout my entire bid here. Kylie, I'm not going back to the life I lived at eighteen. I want more for myself and I will achieve everything I set out to do."

Kylie let the conversation go and I was glad she did. She pulled into the parking garage of the mall and Kylie turned the car off. We got out, walked inside, and I was like a kid in a candy store. The first place I headed was to the Apple store to get a phone. It was time for me to get connected with my people in Chicago.

***

Kylie wouldn't allow me to swipe my own card no matter how many times I told her I had it. She said I deserved to have a fresh start and she was going to make sure she provided it. The bitch surprised me because she gave me unlimited access to the life she lived. Kylie bought designer everything from purses to luggage. The clothes and shoes she purchased were pieces I wouldn't have bought with my own money. She got me an iPhone 14 and a Macbook Pro laptop with all the accessories to go along with them. I tried to stop her, but she was having fun, so I let her do what she felt was right.

Three hours later, we were in my room at the Hyatt Regency. I placed my clothing in the drawers and hung the rest in the closet since I wasn't boarding the plane until Monday, leaving Kylie to take a shower. It felt good to have my independence back and not having to share a bathroom with anyone. I could tell the quietness was going to be a Godsend because it had been a while since I could sleep without any worries.

I washed my hair along with my body several times to get the smell of the halfway house off me. The cleanest place in that house was my room and I hated that shit with a passion. Now, I didn't have to worry about picking up behind anyone because I wasn't going to be sharing my space with another muthafucka, ever. After cleansing myself thoroughly, I stepped out of the shower and dried off immediately. My soul felt refreshed, rejuvenated, and at peace. Knowing I didn't have to check in anymore was all I'd been waiting for. I bowed my head and thanked God for guiding me through ten years of turmoil.

"Thank you, Lord, for keeping me sane. I saw so much in that place, and without you, I would still be there. My mental is in check, and I pray you will continue to lead me in the right direction. I will fuck up, my bad… *mess up* along the way, but that's where you come in, Lord. I need you because you got me this far. You will have to set a few passes aside for me, though. There are a couple things I need to do before I commit to this newfound journey. I know. I know. What I said was a little contradictory and I get it. I have to handle these things, then I'm gon' do right. Don't judge me, though. In Jesus' name, amen."

I had to end that lil prayer because I was fuckin' shit up with the Lord and I didn't want to be on his bad side. Telling the truth was the way to go because Cheese was gon' see me and I didn't believe our reunion was going to be sweet. I hurried to get dressed as fast as I could. I'd had Kylie waiting long enough. We were going out for dinner, and she was also going to take me by the dealership before Mr. Christopher left for the day. Being at a hotel closer to the airport, it was best for me to do all my running around that day because I just wanted to relax alone for once before I went back to Chicago.

The denim shorts and royal blue crop top I chose to wear fit my body like a glove. My abs were on full display, making me blush at what I saw in the mirror. It had been so long since I showed my assets, and I was loving what I'd done with myself. Looking down at my toes, I loved the white polish I chose when Kylie took me to get a manicure and pedicure. I tidied up the bathroom and entered the main room to put on my sandals. Kylie was relaxing as she looked out the window at the lake. The view I had was beautiful.

"You almost ready to get out of here?"

"Yeah, I just have to style my hair in a simple ponytail. I'm not trying to do too much with it."

"Here, I want to give you this." Kylie handed me a thick white envelope which piqued my curiosity.

Slowly opening it, my mouth opened in shock as I sifted through the bills inside. Looking up at her I smiled. "Thanks, but I can't take this. You've done enough for me already."

"Honey, you will take that five grand and put it away with whatever money you have saved for your shop. I want to see you win out here."

I hugged Kylie tightly while fighting the urge to cry. The money jump-started my journey and I was grateful. Stepping back while holding the envelope tightly, all I could do was shake my head. After locking the money in the safe, I went to work on my hair.

It took a good five minutes to do my hair before we were out the door. I felt weird carrying the Louis Vuitton purse on my shoulder. To be honest, I felt so free and feminine. The moment we stepped off the elevator, my ass was turning heads left and right. There were many hellos causing me to wave in response but never stopped walking.

"You got all the boys drooling over you, Miss Honey. I don't blame them because you are wearing the hell out of them shorts. Sis, you have hidden your body far too long for the world to see. It won't be long before you have a man staking claim."

"Believe me when I tell ya, I'm not worried about entertaining anyone. If it doesn't make money, the shit won't make sense. In other words, I'm on a paper chase and it will all be earned by me."

"I'll give you thirty days before somebody's son has his way with you. Honey, you are a woman that hasn't been laid in years. Just let a fine ass man knock the cobwebs out of that box."

"Shut up, Kylie." I laughed. "I have to scope out the scene. First of all, I was a teenaged girl the last time I was in these streets. The game has definitely changed. Then on top of that, the niggas have really lost their minds according to the news segments I've seen on TV. They're killing women then themselves because they don't know how to let go."

"You have a point there. Anyway, I still think you should get that one nut out of the way. Just to put that out there. On another note, where are we going first? To eat, or the dealership?"

"To the dealership," I said as we walked across the parking lot.

The drive to the dealership was twenty minutes. I took that time to set up my phone then attached my debit card to the wallet. After playing with some of the features, I found myself downloading social media sites. Surprisingly, I remembered my login information and just like that, I was back to the bullshit without even trying. There were posts on my page with many saying Happy Birthday to me back in May. I smiled because folks still thought of me even though I wasn't on social media. I left my page and my fingers did the walking by going straight to Cheese's profile. Curiosity got the best of me. I had to see what had him so occupied that he just said fuck me after I didn't turn his ass in for a lesser sentence. The first post told me all I needed to know.

Makin' Chedda Hawkins:14 hrs ago

I need y'all to stop what ya doing and help me wish the love of my life a Happy Birthday. Baby, for the past eight years you have been everything I've hoped for. It's yo' day and you can have whatever you like. The best is yet to come. I love you forever, baby.

There were several pictures of Cheese and "the love of his life". I chuckled when I realized who the woman was. Letty was my best friend in high school. When you saw me, you saw Letty, and vice versa. The thing that fucked me up was, from my understanding, Letty couldn't stand Cheese. She used to express how much he wasn't good for me and made it her business to tell me whenever she saw a bitch grinning in Cheese's face. Thinking back on the distain Letty had for that nigga, she was probably fuckin' him before I took the charge. It was cool because her ass had some explaining to do and was now added to my hit list.

"What you doing over there? You zoned out on me but it's okay."

Lifting my head, I noticed we were off the highway and mere minutes away from the dealership. I was too caught up in my thoughts that I'd left Kylie to endure the ride alone. It wasn't intentional, but I had to act as if I wasn't heated about what I'd just seen.

"I setup my phone. The features are better than before. I don't know if I want to do the face recognition thing though."

"It's convenient, actually. I mean, you trust it enough to give access to your money. Why not your face?"

Kylie actually had a point, so I went ahead and set that up as well. She pulled in front of the dealership and Mr. Christopher was exiting the building. I quickly got out of the car and he smiled while giving my body a once over.

"Honey, is that you?"

"It's me." I smiled back at him. "I told you I would be stopping by. Today was a better day for me since I'm staying out by the airport until my flight on Monday."

"Well, let me go inside and grab your parting gift." He walked back to the door and opened it partially before turning his head in my direction. "You look good. Not to say you weren't beautiful all along, but seeing you in regular clothes brings out the best in you. Keep that persona, Honey. It fits you well."

Mr. Christopher was hitting on me on the low. He could've got it had he pursued me before I was ready to bounce. He was forty-five and handsome as ever. The waves in his head could make you dizzy if you looked too long. He had one deep dimple on the right side of his cheek that even his full beard couldn't hide. Standing at six feet three inches, Mr. Christopher wore the hell out of a suit every day, and the print in the front left nothing to the imagination. I would've said fuck being celibate for him any day. There's truth to the saying, *a closed mouth don't get fed.* He missed out.

I took the time I waited for Mr. Christopher to come back out to call my cousin Cheno to bring him up to date on what was going on. He was pissed when I told him I had to go live in a halfway house for a year. Cheno was my cousin on my father's side. When I was going through hell with my mama and James, he was living in Georgia, but moved back to Chicago two years after I was sentenced. I hadn't seen him in years before I was locked up. Cheno was fifteen, three years older than me, and his sister Breeze was ten. She was the little sister I never had and I loved on her as much as I could until they moved.

Cheno had gone by my mama's house to surprise me and the things she said had him heated. He wasted no time tracking me down in the system and had my back ever since. When Cheese stopped coming to visit, Cheno made sure to show his face twice a month. We talked on the prison phone often and that alone kept me in there levelheaded. Dialing his number, I listened as the phone rang. It seemed like I would be getting his voicemail until the last moment.

"Who this?" Cheno asked.

"Who you want it to be, negro?" I laughed.

"Honey? Where the hell you calling me from?"

"This my number. Lock me in, Cuz. I wanted to let you know I'll be on a flight home Monday. My flight is expected to get in around two in the afternoon. You coming to scoop me up?"

"And you know this, mannnnnnn! My nigga about to touch down!" Cheno yelled in my ear.

"How often you gotta check in with them muthafuckas?"

"I don't. I've done my time. Now, I'm about to get to the bag with no repercussions. I just need to lay low at yo' spot for a minute until I get on my feet. Is that cool?"

"I got you, Honey. I've had shit in motion for you since the day you were released from the prison. The past year just gave me more time to perfect everything. You gon' be straight, Cuzin. That's on my mama."

Aunt Janice passed away three years prior from colon cancer. The shit hurt Cheno to the core because he did all he could to keep his mother on this earth, but all the money he provided for her health care wasn't enough to save her. The doctors did all they could but ultimately, she lost the battle. The day I called him, Cheno could barely talk. I didn't hear from him for three months because he was fucked up behind losing his mother. I understood and became his support system from the inside. Mr. Christopher emerged from the dealership so I had to end the call.

"Thanks for everything, Cheno. I owe you my life for how you've held me down. I'll call you when I get back to the hotel. I'm taking care of some last-minute things."

"Okay, but let me tell you this before you go. You don't owe me shit. You are my family, and your dumb ass mama left you alone to drown. I did what I had to do in order for you to survive in that place. That won't stop now that you free. We about to do big things, baby. Trust me. Send me your flight information and I'll be waiting outside soon as you come out. I love you, Cuz."

"I love you too. Talk to you later."

Fucking me with his eyes, Mr. Christopher stood in front of me but a few feet away. The way he licked his lips had my pussy thumping like a happy rabbit. I slipped my phone in my back pocket and pushed off the car.

"Was that your man you expressing your love to, Miss Honey?"

Shaking my head no while blushing, I put all my weight on my left leg and waited for him to say something else. His jealousy was on full display, but it was little too late for him to show interest in little ole me. When he didn't open his mouth to speak, I went ahead, verbally answering his question.

"Nah, that was me touching basis with my cousin. Tell me this, Mr. Christopher, why are you trying to shoot your shot now?"

"I've always kept you in my line of sight, Miss Love. I'm not the type of guy who mixes business with pleasure and I seemed to have missed my shot with you. But it's my loss and there's nothing I can do to redeem myself. You're heading to Chicago and I'm here in Seattle. That would never work. You're too beautiful for a long-distance relationship, right?"

"To be honest, I don't know how to handle any relationship at this time. I've been confined to an institution for the past nine years. The number one thing in my foresight is getting to know who I am on the outside again. Things have truly changed from when I was out in the world before, and rolling solo is my agenda for now."

"That's understandable. The man who gets his hands on you will be one lucky guy." He paused, admiring me a little more. "I know you have to get going, here's a little something for you to begin your new journey, plus the week's pay I promised. I want you to always believe in yourself, Honey. You deserve everything that's coming your way. Stay on the right side of the law, and the rest will come to you with ease. If you ever need me, I will be there for you."

Mr. Christopher opened his arms for a hug and I walked right into them. His hard chest felt good against my soft body. Not to mention, the aroma of his cologne was swooning me in the worse way. I knew it was time for me to back away from him before I went against everything I'd said to him about being alone for a while.

"Take my personal number. In case you need me, of course."

Nodding, I pulled my phone from my pocket, tapping the screen. I unlocked the phone by placing it in front of my face. I handed it to him and watched as he input his phone in the contacts.

"I'm the first man to grace this phone. That's a sign." He smiled.

"Give me my phone," I said snatching it back. "I will stay in touch with you, Mr. Christopher.

Thank you." I took the envelope from his hand, giving him another hug. I just wanted to get a good whiff of his scent before parting ways.

Giving me one last tight squeeze, Mr. Christopher finally unhanded me. "Drop that Mr. Christopher stuff. We no longer work together. Call me Derrick."

"Aight, Derrick. Take care and thanks for everything. I mean that from the bottom of my heart. You really looked out for me."

"No problem. It was my pleasure grooming you into a better mechanic who will be a successful boss in due time. If you play your cards right, you will have your business up and running before you know it. Soon as you accomplish your goals, I want to know about it."

"I got you. Goodbye, Derrick."

Derrick waved at me as I got in the car. I hurried and closed the door, waving goodbye. He backed away slowly while licking his lips as Kylie backed out of the parking space.

"Damn, Mr. Chistopher is fine!" she said hitting the steering wheel.

"That he is. I had to let him know I wasn't trying to pursue anything with anyone."

"Why did you say that? Girl, you could've got a nut off before you got up out of here. He was the perfect candidate to blow your back out!"

I laughed because the way Kylie glared at me was hilarious. She was more worried about my pussy than I was. There was no way I was going to be sexually involved with my former boss. In due time I was sure someone would pique my interest and I was going to give them the ride of their life. I took that opportunity to examine the contents in the envelope Derrick had given me. Inside there was a check for three thousand dollars plus a twelve-hundred-dollar check for the week. Derrick must've added commission because my weekly salary was never that much without it. I didn't know how he pulled it off and I wasn't about to question his generosity. I was going to electronically send both checks to my account as soon as I got back to the hotel.

Chapter 4

Cheno

The day had finally come for Honey to step foot back on Chicago soil. I was doing a walkthrough of the home I'd purchased for her. Muthafuckas was stuck on stupid if they thought I was going to have her living with me. Nah, the way my pockets were set up, my cousin was going to live life the same way I did out here. When she was supposed to walk out of those prison gates, I already had everything set up for her.

I called my realtor and told her to find me a three-bedroom home in the same subdivision I lived. It was lucky for her to be able to find a house two blocks away. I made it my business to furnish the whole crib from top to bottom. Honey wasn't the same kid that used to run around with me through the southside streets so I didn't know what she would like to eat. The refrigerator was full nonetheless and she would have to make do with what I'd put in there for now.

She had a pool in the back with any and everything she would need to relax and throw a party if that's what she wanted to do. My girl Charlie helped with the interior decorating and she also shopped for Honey. Charlie and my sister Breeze had been all in, helping me with this surprise. I wasn't shit for not filling them in on Honey's homecoming.

My phone rang and I groaned out loud. "What's up?"

"We got a problem, Cheno."

"Handle that shit! I told you I would be off the grid for the day."

"Yeah, I know but this got a lot to do with yo' money. Lil' Mike's cash is short-short. He said he was robbed."

Glancing down at my watch, it was eleven thirty. Honey wouldn't get in for another three hours, so I had time to deal with this punk muthafucka. Anybody that worked with me knew they didn't have to steal nothing because I made sure everybody ate. "Y'all at the trap on the Nine?"

"Mmhmm. Me and Free got him here, shaking in his boots."

"Aight, give me about thirty minutes and I'll be there."

Mike was my top distributor at that particular trap. So, to hear he was robbed didn't sit well with me. I was willing to hear him out, but I was prepared to send him to hell too. Hopefully, his young ass had an explanation with solid proof. It was the only way he would come out of the situation breathing.

After locking up Honey's crib, I jumped in my ride and pushed the pedal to the expressway. Traffic was light so it took me half the time to pull up to the trap. All eyes were on me as I stepped out of my whip. A couple of my workers stood, straightening out their clothes, hiding drinks, and blunts from my view like I gave a fuck about that. They were worried about the wrong shit, and that was my business being robbed.

"Cheno, what's up?"

"You good, Boss?"

Nodding, I walked right pass they ass because my problem wasn't with them. Yet. Soon as I opened the door, Lil Mike jumped to his feet trying to explain himself. Free, my right hand, hit him hard in the chest, knocking the wind out of him. Lil Mike landed on the couch groaning as he doubled over, rubbing the area to soothe the pain.

"Don't get the fuck back up either, nigga." Free sneered standing over him.

"Cool the fuck out, Free." I glared at him. The shit he was on was too excessive in my eyes.

Yes, the trap was robbed, but I knew this was Mike's first mishap and I wanted to hear him out. "Come take a ride with me, Mike."

Mike looked at Free as he slowly stood to his feet. My words held weight when heard, but the way Free was mugging Mike, I wasn't so sure if he would keep his composure. He inched out of Free's reach and made his way over to where I stood. Free's chest heaved and he had a grimaced expression on his face. At nineteen, Mike shouldn't have been as shook as he was. He got down in the streets but acted pussy when it came to a boss nigga.

"I got him, Free. Be cool." I reiterated.

"Cheno, you better kill that nigga!" Fredo snapped from the doorway of the bedroom. "Cut his muthafuckin' hands off or something! There's too much product and money missing in this muthafucka."

"I'm gon' handle this shit on my end. I need y'all to see exactly what was taken and how much.

The inventory and count sheets are in the safe. Stop reacting off impulse and allow me to handle the situation my way. Can y'all do that?" I didn't even wait for a response before leaving the building with Mike leading the way.

The same niggas were nervously outside looking over their shoulders for me instead of the law. Pointing toward my ride, I told Mike to wait for me inside. Once the fiends went to beam up to Scottie, I was on them muthafuckas' asses. "I want y'all to hear me and hear me good. There will be no more drinking or smokin' while on my time! Where the fuck were y'all when somebody ran up in my shit?"

"I-I got caught up with my daughter. Her mammy——"

"Nigga, I don't want to hear yo' whole life story! You know damn well what day pick up is!" I fumed. "Money in this muthafucka by the boat load and only one worker on deck is a fuckin' no go! All you niggas eat good and being here is a priority. Since my shit is irrelevant to y'all, working for free the next seven days shouldn't be a problem either, right? That's what's about to go down and every one of y'all better be here with bells on. Don't like it, speak on that shit now!"

Nobody uttered a vowel, but I meant what I said. I wasn't dishing out a dollar to none of them and I dared any one of them to come for me after the fact. I walked to my whip leaving them standing where they stood. I opened the door and paused, giving them a chance to say what was on their mind. When it didn't happen, I got in and pulled the fuck off. Mike was sweating like he had walked three miles in the desert and the AC was on full blast. His left leg bounced uncontrollably while he picked imaginary lint off his shirt.

"What happened, Mike?" I asked without taking my eyes off the road. "It would be in your best interest to tell the truth from beginning to end."

"Cheno, I'm sorry——"

"First and foremost, I need you to stop bitchin' up when you talkin' to me. Ain't no muthafuckin' pussies on my team. Nigga, yo' voice crackin' and you got tears in yo' eyes. If you want me to murk yo' ass because of that weak shit you doing right now, keep that shit up! Now, cut to the chase and tell me what the fuck happened," I snapped, glancing over at his soft ass.

"Fuck yo' sorry. All I want to hear is the major components of where and who got my bread! Yo' life depends on it."

I reached over Mike and opened the glove compartment then grabbed my piece. Placing it in my lap, I gave the e-way my undivided attention as I waited for him to tell me what I needed to know. Whoever was behind this shit was stupid as fuck because I wasn't to be fucked with and they picked the deadliest way to find out firsthand.

"I got to the trap about seven this morning so I could have everything in order for pick up. I had the counters out and was running the money through when I heard the front door open then close. It was on me for leaving the door unlocked. Ease called and said he was coming through around the same time as me, so I thought it was him coming in." Lil Mike dropped his head in his hands, sighing hard.

"Hold yo' muthafuckin' head up, nigga!"

Repositioning himself in the seat, Mike continued. "When-When I walked out of the back room after Ease didn't come where I was, a big, burly nigga stood in the middle of the living room with his tool aimed at my head. Cheno, I wasn't prepared for that shit. I left my burner in the room."

"Did you recognize the muthafucka?"

"Yeah. His name is Tank."

The name didn't ring a bell to me, but it was obvious Mike knew exactly who the nigga was. My only concern was how he knew Tank, and where the fuck could I find him. Whenever I found him, he was going to wish he'd found another trap to steal from.

"Where can I find him and why did he target my shit?"

"I don't know where he lays his head, but I do know he runs with them westside niggas off Independence," Mike said without hesitation. "If I'm not mistaken, Tank is kin to this dude named Cheese. I'm surprised he's out here robbing muthafuckas because Cheese got the westside on lock and he's making money hand over fist."

The name Cheese was one I was all too familiar with. He was the reason Honey did damn near a decade in the joint. I'd seen his pussy ass on occasions in the club, but never exchanged words with the nigga. Cheese's operation was booming just as mine and I couldn't put a finger on why his family wanted to come for me in the manner he had. Cheese didn't know my relation with Honey and I kept it that way for these types of reasons alone. To keep her out of bullshit.

I'd watched how Cheese moved since I relocated to Chicago. After everything Honey told me I had to witness for myself that his ass was holding his end of the bargain he has with her. He wasn't. According to Honey, Cheese stopped looking out for her years prior and I knew why. Cheese was in a full-blown relationship with a bitch who called herself Honey's best friend. I held the information to myself because it was the last thing my cousin needed to worry about while incarcerated. Now that she was coming home, I would tell her everything I knew.

"There's something I should tell you," Mike said interrupting my thoughts. Without being prompted, he continued. "Ease may have been working with Tank. Don't quote me on that, I'm not sure. Ease said he was on his way but he never showed up. To be honest, he has been talking about not making enough money working with you. His baby mama put him on child support recently and he was awarded to pay six hundred a month."

That information was important for me to know because I didn't even peep that Ease wasn't present at the trap when I arrived. To know he was struggling with a six hundred dollar a month child support payment was baffling. Ease took in a grip weekly and I knew for sure the only bills he had to pay were his car note and half the bills at his mama's crib. Other than that, the nigga should've been straight on funds. If and only if Ease fucked up his money, all he had to do was come talk to me and I would've looked out for him.

"I'm taking in everything you've said, Mike. If you were involved in anyway, I'm personally going to end yo' life. You on probation until further notice. That's the least I can do for now because I need to first find out how much profit I lost and to verify your story. The only reason I haven't acted on impulse is really off the strength of the work you've put in and the loyalty you have shown since I put you on."

Running my hand down my face, I was going against my better judgement by letting Mike go. The shit could blow up in my face or work out in my favor. I really didn't know and was willing to toss the coin. Betting on my damn self.

"I'm going to drop you off at the crib. Lay low until I reach out to you. The moment I have to come looking for yo' ass, you may as well say a final prayer. Understood?"

"I'm sorry all this shit happened, Cheno. I had nothing to do with this. I swear," Mike said sincerely.

"Time will tell. In the meantime, in between time, I'll have yo' whip delivered to yo' spot. Be available when I hit yo' line."

I continued on the expressway toward Mike's crib. I glanced on the dashboard at the time and realized I had less than forty-five minutes to get Honey from the airport. It wasn't shit because Mike lived about fifteen minutes from where I needed to be. As I drove there was nothing but evil thoughts running through my head. Muthafuckas wanted to play with my intelligence at the wrong time, but they were going to learn my cool demeanor wasn't my only trait. On the dark side lived a nigga no one in the Windy City wanted to fuck with on any level.

**

Traffic was hectic at the airport. I hated doing pickups because security made sure you weren't sitting for a long period of time without picking up anyone. I was getting frustrated because I saw everybody except Honey. Her plane had landed and maybe she got caught up at baggage claim. I'd circled around three times when I saw a caramel cutie standing away from the crowd by herself. I couldn't keep my eyes off her and found myself driving my car in her direction as my phone rang.

"Where you at, Cuz?" I asked taking in baby girl's curves.

Her ass was sitting right in a pair of denim shorts. Her abs were chiseled as if she was a personal trainer by trade, legs toned to perfection, and she was beautiful as fuck. I could tell her hair was all natural and pulling it while stroking her inner walls from behind was the image I envisioned.

"Cheno, did you hear me?"

"Nah, my bad. I was kind of distracted. Look, come to the far end of the walkway on the outer side of the airport. That's where I'll be hollerin' at this pretty young thang in a yellow crop top with denim shorts on."

The line went silent but my attention was still on the target. Jealousy kicked in as I noticed my future woman was on the phone. I had plans of blowing up her spot as I stopped in front of her. Rolling down my window, I licked my lips as I scanned her frame from her feet to her face.

"Thirsty ass nigga! I know damn well you ain't lusting over your own fuckin' cousin," Honey snapped. I could hear the words echoing in my ear and I was embarrassed as hell.

"I didn't even know that was you." I laughed hanging up the phone.

Throwing the car in park, I pressed the release button for the trunk and got out to help her with the luggage. Honey stood with a scowl on her face as I embraced her with a hug. She didn't hug me back and I couldn't blame her. My creep ass was ready to risk it all for my own flesh and blood. Honey pushed me off her and stepped back.

"I'm telling Charlie you out here in these streets fuckin' around." Honey looked to her left and rolled her eyes. "Get my bags cause here comes that damn rent-a-cop who has been harassing folks since I walked out here."

Honey had three pieces of luggage and the shit made me wonder how the fuck she had the time to shop while her moves were being clocked. Her ass had some explaining to do because the money I put on her books wasn't enough to have Louis Vuitton luggage. I could only imagine what was inside. Honey got in on the passenger side of my whip and as I lift my foot to sensor the trunk to close, security approached me.

"You have three seconds to move along before I ticket your vehicle." I turned around and came face to face with his fat ass.

"And you got two point five seconds to get the fuck away from me. You just saw me load her bags and now you over here talking shit. How about you go back down there and patrol the other cars that's just sitting curbside with their hazard lights on." I walked to the driver side of my car and saw him entering something into his handheld device. "I'm telling you now, Richard," I said reading the name tag on his shirt. "If I get a ticket in the mail, I'm making a special trip to whoop yo' ass. So, think about what you doing before submitting that shit."

I got in my ride and pulled off. Honey was buckled in while listening to Megan Thee Stallion's

"Hot Girl Summer". I usually didn't allow that female anthem in my vehicle but I was gon' let her make it since it was her first day officially free. I cruised through the southside streets until I hit the expressway. Honey reached out and turned the volume down on the radio then turned slightly in the seat.

"Where's Charlie? Why didn't she come with you to pick me up?" Just as she asked that question my phone rang and Charlie's name appeared on the radio screen. "Oh my God! I just talked her up. Please let me answer the phone," Honey said excitedly holding her hand out.

"Nah, I'm gon' let her be mad until we get to her. She is about to blow my shit up." I laughed as I kept driving. "You will see her in about fifteen minutes so relax. I'm actually taking you to see your first welcome home gift. I know you didn't think you were about to come home and the spotlight wasn't gonna gleam on the brightest diamond. Hopefully, you're not tired because today is your day, Cuz."

"What the hell you got up your sleeve, Cheno?"

"Just wait and see. I said I had you, and I meant that shit from the bottom of my heart. I listened, took notes, and made shit happen. Honey, your world stopped for the past ten years and you grew up in the system. You're out now. The world is yours and you are about to get into the bag. Trust me."

I allowed Honey to wonder what I had in store for her. The way I was feeling inside was a feeling I hadn't felt in a long time. The first time I felt this way was when I made my first million and that was for me. To be able to make sure my cousin was straight through all of her trials and tribulations made me feel like a fairy Godfather. Honey went away a young girl and came out a grown woman. Her life was just beginning, but I was going to stand by her side to watch her soar.

Chapter 5

Charlie

See, Cheno wanted to play on my top by not answering his phone. He'd been moving funny as hell for the past couple of days. Being secretive wasn't the only thing that rubbed me the wrong way. Cheno's lil hoe thought it was sweet to approach me about his infidelities and got swept through the muthafuckin' mud. I called his ass so he could check the bitch, but I guess he wanted his ass whooped, too.

The life I lived since being released from prison was one I never imagined. Going to prison for felony assault was something I wasn't proud of, but I would do it again if that meant protecting myself. The fight I was involved in escalated quickly when a group of females jumped me at a club over a nigga I didn't even know. I ended up breaking a beer bottle and cutting one of them across the face. I was handcuffed and taken to the station where I sat until my hearing. The judge sentenced me to five years in prison and I was shipped to Seattle, Washington to serve my time.

Honey was put in the cell with me and we clicked right away. I'd been incarcerated two years before she arrived so, I had already proved I wasn't to be fucked with on the block. Honey on the other hand was fresh meat and bitches were on the prowl. The two of us fought tooth and nail until she too made a name for herself. I watched Honey grow from a timid teenager to a beast, then a protector for the ones she cared about.

Honey spoke of me to her cousin Cheno as if we were family. He became curious of the person she talked so fond of and told Honey to give me his information. Cheno and I became pen pals and started communicating on the phone and through JPay. Cheno made my days in prison go by rather quickly. We made plans to be together during that time, but I didn't believe Cheno would follow through with any of them once I was released.

Originally from Indianapolis, Indiana, I never thought about moving to Chicago. That's exactly where I ended up a week after I was released. My parents basically disowned me for going to prison even though what I did was in self-defense. They refused to allow me to live in their home. The only thing my mother allowed me to do was use her phone to call someone to come get me off her property. I called my good friend Brittany who opened her home to me.

The first couple of days the two of us caught up on each other's lives then I started noticing Brittany sneaking off into her room frequently as well as picking at her arms and face. I knew the signs of drug abuse, but I'd never known my girl to be into none of that shit. The picture started to become clearer when I went out to look for work a few days later. When I returned, Brittany and her boyfriend was sitting on the couch smoking meth like their lives depended on it. I was fresh out of jail and had no plans of going back on drug charges. I packed my shit, leaving Brittany's house fast as I could.

I wandered around for about an hour before I went to a McDonald's to get something to eat. There was no one I could call because my parents had talked to the entire family instructing them to leave me on the street. I took a gamble by asking the cashier if I could use their phone. I called Cheno explaining what was going on and he told me he would be there in four hours. Six years later, we were still an item. Whatever that meant.

Cheno was everything I wanted in a man. When we were together. Behind my back, the nigga was as single as a dollar bill. With his good looks, deep pockets and a third leg that had gold on the tip, Cheno had females all in his face everywhere he went. When I spoke on it, he brushed the shit off saying he was with who he wanted. Cheno's words said a lot, but his actions said way more. The bitches coming out about what he'd done for them, or how they had been with him the nights he claimed to be working. Not to mention the social media posts some had the nerve to tag me in, but deleted them immediately afterwards. We stayed arguing because of his stupid ass and I was ready to throw in the towel. I was straight financially and didn't need his ass at this point. My heart wanted him though and that's where the confliction came in.

"Charlie, the three o'clock appointment is running late. I just finished the Audi and the owner is pleased with the results."

Taz walked toward me wiping her hands on a rag. Nodding, I tried calling Cheno again, but got the same result, his voicemail. The look on my face must've told Taz all she needed to know.

"Come on, Charlie. What the hell is going on now?"

I put my phone in the back pocket of my coveralls and walked around in a circle. Taz grabbed me by my shoulder and made me face her. My blood was boiling because I was so mad. When I left for lunch, I had no plans on throwing hands with nobody. All I wanted was a burrito bowl from Chipotle then get back to the shop even though I wanted to take my ass home. I couldn't wait for Honey to get out because running shit with her was going to be ten times better than doing the shit alone.

"I went to Chipotle for lunch and ran into that hoe Olivia. She talked mo' shit than a little bit and I ended up moppin' the ground with her ass. I'm so tired of these jealous ass bitches! To top the shit off, Cheno ain't answering his phone and always wonder why I'm forever down his muthafuckin' throat."

"Speaking of the devil, here's your chance to get all that off your chest."

I watched as Cheno parked a few cars down from the entrance and noticed there was a bitch in the car with him. I stormed in his direction and Taz grabbed my arm trying to stop me. Shrugging her ass off, I continued to the driver side of his vehicle and pulled the door open.

"This why you couldn't answer my phone calls, Cheno?" I asked motioning to the passenger seat. "You got some nerve pulling up to my place of business with a hoe in the muthafuckin' car. It's all good though. I'll have yo' shit packed at the door for you to get the fuck out of my house!"

Cheno sat in the seat smiling as if I was a joke. The bitch sat silently before I heard her ass snicker. That shit pissed me off and I pivoted to snatch her ass out by her damn weave. Before I could get to the back end of the car, Cheno jumped out wrapping his arms around my waist.

"Calm yo' ass down. Why you always trying to fight some damn body, Charlie?" Cheno had the nerve to ask.

"Because you don't know how to keep yo' dick in yo' pants! I just had to beat the fuck out of one of yo' hoes and I'm sure she called yo' black ass and told you all about it. Then you have the nerve to bring a new bitch to my muthafuckin' spot! Nigga, you done lost all the brain cells you were born with. Let me the fuck go!"

I struggled to get out of his hold to avail. The passenger door opened slowly causing me to turn the fuck up even more. Scratching at Cheno's hands, I was determined to get away to stomp the hell out of the bitch who was bold enough to get out of the car. When she stood from the car, I got madder because the hoe's shorts had her ass cheeks on display and I knew Cheno had fucked her at some point. She was too eager to be seen. The bitch turned around and that's when I stopped struggling and Cheno released me.

"Honey!"

I screamed running straight into her arms. We hugged each other tightly rocking side to side with tears streaming from our eyes. I hadn't seen my girl outside of the prison walls and she looked good as fuck. My jealousy subsided but my anger for Cheno was put on the back burner for the time being.

"I've missed you so much," I said standing back, taking all of her in. "Why didn't you tell me you were coming home?"

"It wasn't on me. I told Cheno what day and time I would get here. He wanted to surprise you. I see that wasn't a good idea." Looking over my shoulder, Honey glared at Cheno shaking her head. "What the fuck you out here doing, Cuz?"

"Giving these bitches something to throw in my face. Yo' cousin out here being a whole man thot and don't know how to keep his shit on the low like a good cheater. All his troubles seem to find its way to my doorstep at every turn. I'm tired of the shit at this point."

"I'm not doing shit with nobody. Charlie, you let these females live rent free in yo' head without proof. If I was going to step out on our relationship, I promise, I would leave your ass first. Do you know how much pussy I turn down out here? Too much, in all honesty. The way you accuse me of shit, based off what is brought to you on social media, makes me want to fuck one of these bitches long and hard to bring your insinuation to fruition."

"Go fuck 'em, then. Come get yo' shit before you do because I still believe you out here living foul. I'm done with all your bullshit."

"Neither one of y'all is going anywhere. Stop all of this back-and-forth shit. Cheno, you better tighten up before you lose a good thing. You ain't gon' miss her 'til she's gone." Honey hugged me again then glanced around. "Which one of these places is yours, Charlie?"

I smiled wide as I got ready to officially guide my girl to the shop. The business wasn't actually mine per se. I was actually keeping it running until the day Honey was released. Just so happened I knew a lot about cars and had learned alongside Honey in prison. The shop was her vision; I was just here to make sure it stayed afloat and generated revenue for its rightful owner.

"I don't have a business here. I own a salon, but I don't need to be there for it to run smoothly. You know I love fixing cars so I'm helping a friend with their custom shop until they get back home."

"Remember when I talked about having my own shop in prison." Honey laughed. "I'm gon' make that happen soon, believe that shit. Charlie, you are still an upstanding friend, I see. That's what's up! You're holding shit down for your homie. I know he appreciates you for that."

"I'm quite sure *she* appreciates everything I've done for her."

"Damn, it's a woman, huh? That's cool. I'm still gon' put her ass out of business." Honey laughed. "I hope you didn't give her any of my ideas, bitch."

"Actually, she brought her ideas to me. Honey, to be honest, she had the same dreams and aspirations as you. Down to the all-woman crew. I'm sorry, but she is doing what you wanted to do. I didn't tell her anything about you."

"I know muthafuckin' well you ain't supporting this shit, Charlie! How am I supposed to top a business that is basically doing what I wanted to do. You know what? I respect you for holding things down for her. I need you to let your boss know that I'm coming harder than she has ever came. Let me see what y'all got going on."

Cheno laughed as I led Honey to the shop and hearing that shit made me remember I was mad at his ass. I had to breathe in order to not lash out on him because without Cheno, this moment wouldn't have been possible for my friend. I had to keep my cool and the shit was hard to do with all the pent-up anger itching to come out.

Cheno got in front of us walking backwards as he recorded Honey as we made our way to my friend's building. The shop took up half of the block and was big ass hell. Cheno had yet to reveal the name of her establishment on the property, but it was ready for its reveal now that Honey was out. As we got closer to the front of the shop, Cheno's smile got bigger.

"Honey, I'm so glad you are out, and I hope you're ready to control these streets with ya' boy. I never wanted you to be directly in the mix with me, but your ideas amazed me every time you expressed your vision to me. I wanted to make sure you would be straight out here." Cheno grabbed hold of the rope that hung high on the covered sign. "I told you from the time you reached out to me that I had your front, back, and in between and I meant that shit. I listened to everything you said down to the color and design and I made that shit happen."

Pulling hard on the rope, the covering fell to the side, revealing the name of the shop. *Customization by Honey* sat boldly on the top of the building in green lettering. Honey stopped in her tracks with her hand over her mouth. She screamed loud as hell as she wagged her finger at me while jumping up and down. I took that opportunity to wave all the girls out of the building so they could meet their new boss.

"Y'all got me! A bitch was lava hot thinking somebody else was in these Chicago streets making money off my shit. Thank y'all so much for bringing my vision to life. And baby, these women are sexy as fuck in overalls and all! I'm lovin' all of this and can't wait to get my hands dirty!"

"Honey, you not putting in work anytime soon. I want you to relax and get comfortable being home. Meet your team though," Cheno said turning to the women sporting their *Customization by Honey* gear.

The first woman stepped forward and Honey's mouth formed into a smile bigger than the one she sported after learning about her establishment. "Breeze?" she asked uncertainly.

Breeze was a spitting image of Cheno in girl form. She smiled at Honey and the first thing anyone ever noticed were the deep dimples in each of her cheeks and her perfect teeth. Standing about five feet nine inches, with a caramel complexion, her faux locs were neatly done sitting on top of her head in a bun protected by a scarf. The way her overalls hug off her frame showcasing her Calvin Klein underwear, one would automatically know Breeze was rooting for the same side as her brother. I didn't give a damn about her sexuality at all, she was beautiful either way. She wore a black tank showing off the half sleeve on her right arm and a full one on her left. Breeze nodded and Honey hugged her tightly around her neck.

"You have grown beautifully from the little ten-year-old I remember. I've missed you so much, boo. What do you do at Honey's?" Honey asked stepping back wiping tears from her eyes.

"I've missed you, too, and I'm sorry I didn't come to visit while you were locked up. A lot has been going on but that's not an excuse."

Honey waved her off giving Breeze another hug. "It's okay. We have nothing but time to catch up."

"Fo' sho. Anyway, I'm your oil master. In other words, I do all the oil changes and any other fluids a car may need. Don't get it twisted, I know how to do it all, but you know, I get in where I fit in." Licking her lips, Breeze chuckled. "I took classes and was certified just so I could work alongside you. When Cheno told me what he was going to do for you, I wanted in."

"Okay, that's what's up. I would rather you work with me than with your damn brother." Honey looked over Breeze's arm and I knew she had spotted the name *Millie Mob* in the detail of her tattoo. "What is Millie Mob, Breeze?" she asked sneering at me.

I stood with a smirk on my face because I wasn't worried about her being upset. That shit was going to last all of sixty seconds.

"It's the name of our biker club. Charlie put it together about five years ago, but we haven't really been active because we were waiting on you."

Honey ran and hugged me again because that was also one of her visions I made happen. She talked about starting a biker club with the name Milie Mob named after Millenium Park. Honey learned how to ride a motorcycle while with Cheese. She had a green Yamaha YZF-R7 before she went to prison. Cheese wasn't coming off that muthafucka. I tried to buy it back from him and he laughed in my face. Wait until Honey sees the upgrade I purchased for her ass, though. She was going to shit bricks.

"You keep making me proud by the minute! Bitch, I love you!" Honey screamed, kissing me on the cheek. "Okay, I gotta get back to my girls. What's your name and what do you do here?" she asked the chocolate beauty standing next in line.

"I'm Tequila. Yes, that's my real name." She laughed. "My mother loved the alcoholic beverage so much and just had to name her one and only daughter that shit. Now, it's all I drink. My technical skills and experience in the automotive field are on point. I took automotive classes at Lincoln Tech and excelled at it. I handle all of your diagnostic needs. I conduct the standard maintenance care as well as provide repair service such as brakes, hydraulics, fuel ignition, air conditioning, and electrical systems of a vehicle. I assist others anyway I can and keep up with the inventory. I'm twenty-six, and it's nice to finally put a face to the name Honey."

Tequila was dark and beautiful. She stood about five feet four inches with a slim waist and an apple bottom booty. Her hair was styled in medium knotless braids that she wore long. All the men that came into the shop always tried to have their way with her, but Tequila wasn't having it. She was one of those girls who knew her worth and the niggas that came at her never came correct. Baby girl was about the bag, and she would hustle every day to provide for herself before she would ever let a nigga play in her face.

I was proud of the team I'd put together because the way Honey's face beamed listening to the girls was picture perfect. She nodded in approval and hugged Tequila before moving on. Taz was my bestie and she had a scowl on her face. I already knew she was in her feelings about the way Honey was getting all of my attention. Any time I talked about Honey coming home, there was a shift in Taz's demeanor. It was something I would have to talk to her about because the last thing she needed was to get fired or her ass whooped for being territorial.

"What's your job here and what's your name?" Honey asked with a smile. Taz sighed heavily and rolled her eyes. Before she could introduce herself, Honey held up her hand. "Is there a problem, ma'am?"

"My grandmother is a ma'am, not me. My name is Tasmeen, but you can call me Taz. I'm your manager." Taz stood with her arms folded over her chest with an attitude.

"Now, Taz, don't start that bullshit."

"Don't start what, Breeze? I introduced myself and that's all I have to say."

Breeze walked up on Taz, whispering in her ear as she held her around the waist. Taz seemed to calm down for a bit, but she still didn't offer an apology for her actions. Nodding to whatever was said to her, Taz made her way into the shop quietly.

"I'm sorry for Taz's attitude, Honey. She's worried about you coming in, taking Charlie from her. They have become real close throughout the years. Taz will come around eventually. Until then, I will make sure she doesn't give you too much attitude."

"I've dealt with plenty of females with the same temperament while in prison. I'll give her the chance to get some act right in her system before I fuck her up. I'm quite sure Taz will come around sooner than later."

"I'm sure she will, too. Aye, If it's alright with you, I'm gon' head out. I'm gon' see you later tonight, though."

"Yeah, that's cool. We'll catch up."

All eyes followed Breeze as she jumped into her blue Camero ZL1. She started her whip and Megan Thee Stallions "Ungrateful" blared out of the speakers. Taz walked back out soon as Breeze pulled out of the parking lot, and I hoped like hell she wasn't going to be on any type of bullshit. I knew firsthand how Honey got down with the best of them and I didn't believe a word she said to Breeze outside of fucking Taz up. To my surprise, Taz didn't say anything but the scowl she wore was still plastered on her face for Honey and everyone else to see.

"If any of you have a problem with me being here, speak now or forever hold your peace. I treat people the way they treat me, and I give out the same energy that I'm given. There will always be an open-door policy for any one of you to come talk about any problems you may have in the shop or personally. I know we don't know one another, but in due time that shall change. My goal is to make this a family environment and it will be us against the world. Animosity is something that will not be tolerated amongst us. This has been my dream for years while I was locked up and it is a blessing for me to have two people that loved me enough to make my dream come true. So far, I'm pleased with the women who were handpicked to help the business strive."

Honey glanced around at the women, waiting for anyone to address any issues they may have. Taz huffed and rolled her eyes but didn't speak on anything. When no one stepped forward, Honey went back to the introductions, pointing at the woman standing before her.

"Hi, Honey, my name is Golden, but everybody calls me Goldie. Welcome home, and I can't wait to work under your guidance. Usually, our team is respectful at all times. I'm going to apologize on behalf of Taz as well."

Taz tapped her foot lightly on the concrete, obviously frustrated. "I don't need anyone to apologize for me."

"Drop the attitude, Taz. You making this shit more than it really is. That's unnecessary," I said, warning her with my eyes. She knew not to clap back at me because I didn't play that disrespectful bullshit.

Goldie lived up to her name with a mane of blonde hair. She was a redbone with a thick frame. She was built like a stallion and stood with confidence. Like all of the other ladies that worked with us, Goldie didn't look like she made a living being a mechanic. She kept a full face of makeup and fresh manicures, regardless of getting dirty five days a week. Goldie was the peacemaker of the crew. She didn't like conflict because she saw a lot of violence growing up in her household. But she wasn't going to allow anyone to get away with disrespecting her or anyone she cared about.

"Thanks for that, Goldie. I can't wait to work with you as well. As for Taz," Honey said giving Taz her undivided attention. "She will come around after she gets to know me as a person. Ain't that right, sista?"

Taz hunched her shoulders and that made Honey chuckle a little bit. I was proud Honey didn't push her to reply verbally. Honey had somewhat changed into the young girl I shared a cell with.

"I see I have met everyone on the team."

"Actually, you haven't. You still have to meet Tiny and Spanky. They had the day off and would've been here had someone told me you were coming home today," I said as a black Denali pulled up to the garage door. "Well, it looks like my last appointment is here. We have work to do, Honey. Go home and I'll see you later. I love you, sis. Welcome home. You and I have so much to catch up on and I can't wait."

"I love you back, Charlie. Thank you for everything. I'll get your number from my knucklehead cousin and text you with mine. One more thing, do not put Cheno's shit on the front lawn."

"Fuck, Cheno!" I said walking away. "I mean that shit disrespectfully."

Chapter 6

Breeze

Chicago was a city of fun, good food, and a lot of fuckin' drama. Even if you stayed in your lane the bullshit would find you. It was the same way in Georgia. When Cheno told me he was moving back to our hometown, I packed up and came with him. There was nothing in Georgia for me since our mother was no longer with us. I lost my faith in the Lord when he took her away from me. My mother and my brother were all I had because my deadbeat ass father never thought to show his face and acknowledge the fact that he had a daughter who no longer had her mother. If he ever decided to reach out, I had a mouthful of disrespect ready to unleash on him.

For someone who left his family to raise someone else's three children and produced two more biologically after he stopped providing for Cheno and I was what made matters worse. The hatred for Dawson Haley grew with each passing day he was absent. Cheno and my mama always told me not to allow his absence to anger me. I couldn't, and took that shit out on anyone who tested me. I was getting in trouble in school and damn near got kicked out until one of my teachers took me under her wing and taught me how to deal with my anger.

My lifestyle was the reason my father shut me out of his life. He couldn't accept the fact that his little girl would never wear the dress, high heeled shoes, and accessories he wanted to purchase for her senior prom. My mind wandered back to that day instantly.

It was my mama's idea to call Dawson to help with my prom. Cheno offered and I declined because I had worked hard to save money for the event. By that time, I had been dating females for two years. I came out to my mama at the age of fifteen and scared was an understatement because I didn't know how she would react to the news. I had witnessed my girlfriend being ridiculed by her entire family when she told them. They called her everything but the Child of God. It was the first time I'd heard the word bulldagger.

Being Christian didn't mean a damn thing in my eyes and for her aunt to call me that shit only pissed me off. I went in on all of them. From young to old. I didn't give a fuck. The things I'd heard about the church they attended, being in a same sex relationship were the least of their worries. After I finished reading their ass about their beloved pastor who was fucking the choir director, the family member who was fucking whoever was down in the church bathroom, and the deacon uncle who was hooked on the booger sugar, I was kicked out and my girl was shipped off to God only knew where.

My mama embraced me and made it clear that she would support me in whatever I decided to do in life. I cried like a baby as I sighed with relief. The harsh words I anticipated never came. Instead, she wiped my tears while telling me how proud she was of me for standing in my truth. Cheno was supportive too but explained about all the backlash I may endure being a lesbian. He said he would have my back if I decided to be a zebra at the zoo. The only person that had a problem was my sperm donor.

Dawson came through with no questions asked. He drove me and my mama to the mall to shop for my prom clothes. As he sifted through the dresses, I strolled to the men's department to check out the suits. My mama was right on my heels because she knew I was not putting on a dress for nobody. *It didn't take long for me to find a black Armani suit with straight legged pants, a royal blue shirt, and a pair of royal blue and black dress shoes that set the suit off perfectly. We went back to the women's section and found Dawson standing with a big smile on his face. I, in turn, frowned at the bright pink halter dress he had draped over his arm. He held it up for me to see and there was no excitement in my eyes. I had been a tomboy most of my young life and that color never did anything for me. My mama tried her best to dress me like a princess, but all I wanted was sweatpants and t-shirts.*

"This would look beautiful on you, Breeze. Go in the dressing room and try it on. You're about a size eight, right?"

To be honest, I didn't know what size I was in women clothing. "I've already found what I'm going to wear. All I need you to do is pay for the items. The dress is cute. It's just not for me."

"What do you mean the dress ain't for you? "Dawson asked.

"Just like I said. I have my own style, and a dress isn't part of it."

I could tell Dawson was pissed. His attention zoomed in on the items my mama held in her hands. His brows furrowed; the frown he wore deepened as he took in the suit, and shoes. "Is Cheno escorting you to prom?"

"No. That's what I'm wearing. I don't want to wear a dress," I explained calmly as I could.

"What woman do you know that wears men suits?" Before I could respond, Dawson continued his rant. "The only ones I know of are those damn dykes!"

My mama looked around nervously because it was like everything in the store came to a standstill. I laughed lowly as I pulled my wallet from my back pocket. There was no use standing around going back and forth with him when I knew he wasn't going to pay for my shit. I took the items from my mama, feeling Dawson watching my every move. When he took a step toward me, he stopped in his tracks when my mama stood in front of him.

"This is not the time nor the place to address this, Dawson. You have everybody in this store waiting to see how this will unfold. Wait 'til we get back to the car."

Dawson took heed to what my mama said and didn't follow me. I swiped my card, grabbed the bags, and walked out of the store. My sperm donor was on my ass. I felt I didn't owe him any type of explanation and didn't have any intentions of giving one either. I knew where the shit was going the moment he said the word dyke. His ass was a true homophobe, and I wasn't with that degrading shit. The two people that meant the world to me accepted me as I was, and that was all that mattered. Dawson could suck the silicone off my strap.

"Breeze, come here, now!" Dawson yelled at my back.

"Go to hell, Dawson." I shot back, never losing my stride. "You picked a fine time to come back and play daddy. As you can see, I didn't need you to pay for nothing. I wasn't the one who suggested you be here. What does that tell you? What I do know is this; the energy you using to come at me, you should've had when you left and said fuck us. At least I would've known you still gave a fuck."

Dawson spun me around by the back of my shirt and we both stared each other down. Standing five feet eleven inches, I got my height from the man who stood before me. A few more inches and we would have been looking each other in the eye. It didn't matter who he was, Cheno instilled in me not to be afraid of no nigga.

"Don't you ever in your life talk to me like that! You are being real disrespectful right now." Dawson seethed.

"And you not? Get the fuck outta my face with that bullshit. In order to get respect, you gotta give it. For the record, I'm that dyke you despise so much."

"Breeze, you are not a dyke—"

"You are correct. I'm a proud lesbian and there is nothing anybody can say nor do to change that. Respect my sexuality because it's here to stay. Then again, maybe this is something else you can use to stay the fuck away from me." I turned to walk away but Dawson wasn't finished.

"How do you know women is who you you're supposed to be with? You're seventeen and probably never even given a boy a try."

Dawson's voice cracked with every word he spoke as if he was on the verge of crying. He was humoring me to the point I couldn't even be mad anymore. I'd never been with a boy and had no desire to test the waters either. I liked what I liked and that was pussy.

"Dawson, Dawson, Dawson. You are correct again. I have never physically experienced the male species. But mentally, you were my experience of what I didn't want in a relationship. The way you cheated, had other children, abandoned and embarrassed my mother, I knew there was no way in hell I would procreate with a nigga. At least with a woman, all the bitch could do was leave my ass. So, thanks for teaching me all about nothing ass muthafuckas."

The flashback somewhat had me in my feelings, but I refused to allow it to take me to a dark place. Dawson chose to stay away from me, and that was fine. There was no coming back, though. He better hope like hell he didn't need me at any given time because I needed him for years and he didn't give a fuck. My thoughts went back to Taz and how she was about to show her ass at the shop. I had to put a stop to that madness because with all the shit Honey had been through, Taz was definitely going to be on the losing end of that battle.

I met Taz when she came in for an interview at the shop. Her beauty was captivating and there was no way I wasn't going to shoot my shot. After her interview, I approached her and asked her out. At first, Taz tried to act as if she didn't like women but I knew better. My gaydar was going off full force. We had one thing in common and that was cars. So, to me that was a start. It didn't take much for me to persuade her to input my number into her phone. Taz didn't call for weeks and I didn't sweat her. The more we were around each other, the stronger the sexual tension built up. Within a few months, Taz was my girl. I knew going exclusive with her was the only way to keep Taz in my life and I swear a muthafucka tried. The shit didn't work for me because my options were still open. Commitment was something I wasn't ready for, and Taz wasn't going for it. Ending things with her was hard, but one thing I wasn't into was purposely hurting females. Taz knew her worth. She refused to settle, and I didn't blame her.

The breakup was hard on Taz because she had to witness female after female coming to visit me at the shop. I wasn't throwing anything in her face purposely, but I could see the hurt it caused her all the same. I tried taking her feelings into consideration and told my dips to stop coming by without calling, but I couldn't control anyone's actions. Taz and I were cool after it was said and done. We didn't have any bad blood between us so it was easy to work together each day.

When my girl Sia would come by the shop, Taz would do petty shit to get under her skin. Not because she was jealous, but because Taz knew I wasn't locked in with Sia either. Besides, we were still doing our own thing on the low despite all the rah-rah she cried about not being the only woman in my life.

Sia's insecurities were at an all-time high at this point and the shit was working my nerves. Taz was always the root of her tantrums. A blind man could see the connection we had when we were in close proximities of each other. I've told Taz to chill on all the bullshit when Sia was around because it was complicating what I had going on with her. I played a major part in our trysts too and it didn't make what I was doing right.

I was driving around aimlessly through the city, smoking while getting lost in my thoughts. The smoke from my blunt filled the interior of my ride like a gas chamber. Many said I was addicted, but in actuality the weed kept me from slapping a muthafucka into the middle of next week. My thought process was fucked up since my mind reverted back in time. I ended up on the southside, in Englewood. It was live at the moment, and I should've been heading further south to the burbs to get some damn sleep instead. That was too much like right for me, though.

While I tried to figure out what I wanted to do with my life once I moved to Chicago, Cheno took care of me and all of my finances. The shit was cool at first, then I felt as if I was a major burden on him. My mama didn't raise me to be weak. I knew I had to get my weight up and take care of my damn self. I badgered Cheno for months to allow me to work for him so I could make some money. He was against the shit from the start, but my persistence finally broke him down enough for him to send me on a test run. Cheno gave me two ounces of weed to see how I would do. That shit was gone within an hour before I was hitting him up for more. He gave me a pound when I pulled up on him and I got that off in a matter of two hours. That was the day my brother realized that I was the female version of him, and it was on from there. I became a full-time cannabis dealer and was damn good at it.

Driving down 59th Street, I turned onto Loomis. All my niggas were out, and I loved to see shit like that. I was going to chill long enough to get some weed off. The block was thick. Soon as I bent the corner, all heads turned. My whip was the focal point every time I showed up. All the work I'd put into my bitch made me proud of the outcome. It wasn't shit to some, but everything to me. I found a spot to park my car and got out.

"Breezy, what up?"

"You know what it is, Coo!"

Coo was my number one buyer and was always ready for my pull up. He made it to my vehicle before I could walk across the street. I opened the door and waited for him to tell me what he wanted.

"Aye, you got two pounds on you? I know I usually get one and I'm gon' apologize for the inconvenience. It's all good if you don't, though. It's some last-minute shit on my part and I understand."

"You talking too fast, muthafucka. Slow yo' roll." I looked at his ass like he was crazy as I hit the button on my key fob. The middle console of my armrest rose up then opened. I always had pounds separated when I came on Loomis because Coo was always ready for whatever. I'd studied his ass for over a year so I knew he got more sometimes; he'd just hit my line beforehand. Grabbing what I needed plus a few sevens and fourteens, I hit the button again to conceal my shit. I reached behind the driver's seat and got a black plastic bag then put his product inside of it.

"That shit was raw as hell. Where the fuck you go to have that installed?"

"First things first, Coo," I said standing up straight. "Give me my money, nigga."

Coo laughed as he dug in his pocket and gave me what was rightfully owed. Me and him never had to discuss payment because he already knew. I counted my bread while holding his bag and that made him laugh harder.

"Breeze, why you always trying to handle me like a sucka? Have I ever fucked you over?"

"Hell nawl, and you won't get the opportunity to do so, either." I smirked. "Don't take that shit personal. I don't trust no muthafuckin' body. You should learn to do the same. The shit may save ya life one day. Good lookin' and nice doing business witcha."

"Yo' ass something else. Now tell me who hooked yo' ride up."

"Oh, I forgot all about that," I said putting the money in the pocket of the shorts I wore under my overalls. "I did that. It's what I do to pay the bills. Come see me at Customizations by Honey. It's on 111th and Stewart. I want you to know now, don't take offense either. The shit ain't cheap. You gotta come correct or don't come at all. As a matter of fact," I said opening the door to my whip again. Taking one of my business cards from the holder attached to my sun visor, I handed it to him. "Hit me up when you're ready."

"Aight. I'm gon' send some business yo' way, too. Come walk with me, though. These niggas think they about to smoke with me but they in for a rude awakening. Make some money, sis."

"Shid, I was gon' do that anyway. Who wants something?" I asked as we walked across the street.

"I'on know. I'm about to find out for you. Go stand on the porch and I'll send them over one by one so it won't draw no attention to you."

Nodding, I walked to Coo's porch and patiently waited while he hollered at his people. My phone was buzzing in my pocket but whoever it was gon' have to wait until I got back in my whip. The last thing I needed was for some shit to pop off and I was caught lackin'. I never had to worry about anything when I came through there. Talking shit to Coo was something I did, but I knew he had my back whenever I was in his presence. I would be straight regardless because I never left the crib without my heat on my hip. I lived by the *wish a muthafucka woods* and I would bury a bitch deep in the dirt if I had to.

A few niggas came up to cop from me and I handed them what they needed like the candy lady at the corner store. A heavyset dude approached, licking his crusty lips and I almost threw up in my mouth. Everybody and their mama knew I liked women of all shades, shapes, and nationalities. But this nigga gave me the feeling that he was about to try and shoot his shot. He wore a pair of white Ones that seen better days, a dirty ass shirt which had ketchup stains on the front, and some black Dickie pants that barely covered his ass. The nigga titties were bigger than mine and two more bitches put together.

"What you trying to get?" I asked looking everywhere but at him before he could get too close.

"Your phone number," he said in his sexiest voice. The shit sounded like he had asthma or some shit. "Then I'll take a tre-five to go."

I chuckled, swiping my thumb across my nose. I had to compose myself so I wouldn't laugh in his face. Looking down, his shoes was the first thing my eyes landed on. My stomach cramped up like a fist from me holding my laugh in. "My number won't be shared with you or any other nigga for that matter. As far as that tre-five, I can't help you with that either. I don't sell that lil' shit."

"What the fuck you mean? You suppose to give your customers what we want, and I want a tre-five!"

"The kids in Ethiopia want food, too, but they have to settle for what's provided, right?" I finally looked him in the face, and if looks could kill. "You could always go elsewhere. I won't be mad atcha."

"Fuck yo' wanna be a nigga ass, bitch! It's yo' loss. I didn't want yo' dike ass no way!" He gritted.

"I've never portrayed myself to be a man a day in my life. I know I'm a woman. Why the fuck am I going back and forth with you about this? Nigga, move around. I don't sell tre-fives and that's that. If you broke, just say that."

"Bitch, my money longer than yours, just like my dick!"

"You sure about that?" I smirked. "Big bank take lil' bank?" I snapped loudly drawing attention.

The nigga was madder than a muthafucka because he was embarrassed by this time. Coo was making his way over to see what the problem was and some of his people followed; knowing I shouldn't put on a show, but his fat ass fucked up bringing up what he didn't know about me. So, what better way to humble his ass than to make him look like the clown he was?

"I'll have yo' ass out here crying like the girl you are if I showed you the money in my pocket. You don't want them type of problems."

"But I do." I laughed. "Put yo' money where yo' mouth is, and when I take yo' money, I want you to show me yo' dick because I bet my shit bigger than yours, too!"

Everybody laughed. If big boy was a cartoon character, he would have smoke coming out his ears. His ass should've known that bullying shit wouldn't work on a real one like myself. So, since he didn't get the memo, I had to put his ass in his place.

"Gone head and take her shit, Bam," Coo said, nudging the nigga with his elbow.

"Just give Coo everything on your person and stop stalling. I'm gon' teach you not to play with women. You gon' have a newfound respect for us after today. I promise."

Bam took money out of both of his pockets and handed it over to Coo. Counting up the funds, Coo's right eyebrow rose a bit before he counted it again. Bam then went in his wallet producing a couple more bills while I stood, waiting with my arms folded over my chest.

"Aight. I know what this man has, now it's your turn, Breeze." I went into my pocket and Coo held his hand up to stop me. "Wait, before I allow this to go any further, y'all need to make this shit clear. Whoever has the most money takes all, right? No bullshit behind this and y'all walk away peacefully."

"Yeah, that's what this shit is about. I'm not a sore loser so I'm ready for whatever," I said truthfully.

"I'm good with that because I know her weak ass don't got more money than me. She about to run across the street to her car like dude did in *Friday* when Debo snatched his chain."

His boys laughed and dapped him up like Bam had already won my shit. I went into my right pocket and handed it to Coo. He went to count it and I shook my head.

"Hold on, there's more where that came from." Presenting another knot from my left pocket, I handed that over too. Then I went into my shorts and gave Coo the money he had given me and smiled. Now you can count that shit up. I'll save him a little bit by not going into my trunk.

Coo finished counting my money and looked over at Bam. His big ass was fuming with his fist balled up. Everybody waited for Coo to give the results quietly.

"Bam, gave me fifteen hundred, right?" Coo asked glancing at Bam. He nodded in agreement. "Okay, Breeze gave me fifty-five hundred and the entire bankroll is hers."

Coo walked up to give me the money and Bam charged the stairs. Before he made it to the top landing, he was looking wide-eyed into the barrel of my Nina. That bitch never disappointed and his ass was about to learn.

"Put the gun down, Breeze. He ain't gon' do shit."

"Nah, Coo, he is about to do something. Pull yo pants down, nigga, and let me see yo' pussy!

I hate a sore loser. Especially one that ain't got no balls." I snatched the money from Coo with my gun still trained on Bam. I peeled off a hundred dollar bill and threw in his face. "I'll leave you with yo' dignity. But go buy a muthafuckin' clue. You gon' need it the next time you approach me."

I walked down the steps not worrying about Bam coming up behind me. My gun was still attached to my hand with my finger on the trigger. I didn't go to the range for nothing, and best believe I never miss.

"Aye, Coo, hit me up when you ready. I won't be coming back because yo' block hot," I shouted over my shoulder as I hit the key fob to unlock my door. I got in, laid my tool in my lap, and drove off with "Represent" by Nas flowing through my speakers.

***

Hitting the expressway, I cruised all the way to Matteson. I loved living out in the burbs, but hated the fact there wasn't as much action as in the city. Cheno was the reason I lived so far out, but I'm not mad at him because he was only looking out for me. My phone cut the music off in the car and I rolled my eyes when I saw my girl Sia's name appear on the screen. I meant to call her back but the shit with Bam took over my thoughts. He was going to be a problem.

"What's up? Why you blowing me up like that?"

"I've been calling you for almost an hour. Where you at?" Sia asked with an attitude.

"Taking care of business. What's the emergency?"

Sia held on to the phone without saying a word. I pulled into the parking lot of the liquor store and got out. A couple of females were coming out laughing loudly. One of them smiled in my face and said *hey, baby*. I ignored her but all Sia heard was what lil mama said.

"Who the fuck you with?"

"Cut that shit out, man. I'm at the damn liquor store. You heard what she said but did you hear me respond? That's what I mean when I tell you about worrying about the wrong shit. You forever accusing me of shit, and I don't even be doing nothing. Fuck around and get what you searching for and it's gon' be a wrap if I find a lil yeah-yeah that don't nag my ass. I'll holla at you when I get to the crib."

I hung up on her jealous ass and went in to get me a fifth of Crown apple and some apple juice. My patience for Sia were growing thin. All I needed was someone that brought peace into my life. The shit I was doing with Taz never caused me to treat Sia any differently. She assumed I was out doing wrong. Little did she know, it wasn't pussy I was in the street chasing; I was running after the bag.

"Will that be all for you?" The cashier asked.

"Yeah."

Paying for my items, I snatched the bag and told ole girl to keep the change. I was tired as hell because I had been up at since six that morning and it was damn near six in the evening. When I got to the crib I had to shower and take a nap quick because there was no way I could miss out on what my brother had planned for Honey. Turning into my driveway, I let out a loud groan because Sia was sitting on my front porch with a plastic cup in her hand. By the looks of things, she probably went by the shop and I wasn't there so she came straight to my spot.

We didn't live together because I wouldn't be able to deal with her questioning me and having to hear the shit every night while trying to sleep. She used to have a key, but I took that shit back when she chose the middle of the night to come over just to see who was in the house with me. Waking up to a muthafucka standing over you could easily end in a homicide. Hell, I think I saved Sia from getting her ass killed.

"What you doing?" I asked soon as my foot hit the pavement.

"I've been sitting out here for hours waiting on you to show up. I went by your job and you weren't there. So, tell me where you been, Breeze."

Sia was out of her mind coming to me with this bullshit. After what Bam tried to pull, I wasn't in the mood to deal with nothing else. I closed the door and walked right pass her ass. While I unlocked the door, Sia continued yapping behind me.

"So, you can't talk now?"

I ignored her and continued on to my bedroom as I peeled my clothes from my body. I stripped down to my boxers and sport bra before throwing the items in the hamper. Slowly walking across the room, I could feel Sia watching my every move from the doorway. Removing a clean set of underwear, a t-shirt, and a pair of basketball shorts from the drawer before heading to the bathroom. She was on my ass like white on rice and it was starting to irk the fuck out of me.

"Stop fuckin' following me! If you gon' stay here, go sit down until I'm finished. When I come out of this bathroom you better have your attitude in check."

Slamming the door in her face, I started the shower before applying my facial cream. After moisturizing my face, I brushed my teeth then got naked. I turned the water on to the temperature of my liking, then stepped into the shower. My muscles relaxed the moment the hot water hit my shoulders. Lathering up my loofah, I washed my body a couple times and rinsed off. As I got out of the tub, I grabbed a towel and wrapped it around my body as the door crept open.

I continued drying my body then skipped the oiling of my skin process. Instead, I hurried and got dressed before walking pass leaving Sia's ass right where she stood. My body was trying to shut down on me. As I got comfortable on my bed, I noticed my money was scattered about and I knew that wasn't how I put it on the dresser. Sia was still looking dumb but she was bound to get choked out if she didn't put my shit back.

"Um, you stealing from me now?"

Sia's eyes ballooned out her head. She closed her eyes quickly hoping I didn't see that shit, but I did. She didn't say anything right away but she didn't have to. The way she fidgeted around told me the bitch did just what I expected. Sia knew better than to touch anything that belonged to me because all she had to do was ask and she shall receive. Actually, her spoiled ass didn't have to open her mouth. I was the type who gave just because and that was the reason I was so pissed off.

"Empty yo' pockets and purse, Sia. If I have to get up and count my shit, it's gon' be worse on yo' part."

When she didn't move, I got out of the bed swiftly and counted my bread just as fast. Sia called herself swiping five hundred dollars off top. Before I could stop myself, I threw the money back on the dresser and yoked her ass up. I had my hands around her neck and saw red. I wasn't one to put my hands on a woman, but this bitch just tried to play on my top.

"Keep that shit!" I gritted in her face. "The shit you pulled ended what we had. If you have to steal from me, there's no telling what else you would do. I hope that five hunnid holds you over because that's all you will ever get from me. Get the fuck out!"

I shoved her into the wall and walked out of the room and to the front door. The sound of Sia's flip flops told me she was damn near running behind me. I stood at the door waiting for her to leave. Instead, of getting the fuck away from me, she stood there with tears running down her face. That shit wasn't moving me and she knew it. Sia opened her mouth but I didn't want to hear nothing.

"Save it, man. No words can change my mind. Go to ya mammy and tell her all about it. Anything I've ever bought for you is yours. Nothing ties us together so you're free to do you."

"Babe——"

"Go, Sia!"

She crossed the threshold and did an about face. I slammed the door hard enough to shake the African art on my walls. She rang the doorbell repeatedly, screaming and trying to kick my shit off the hinges. I went to my room, got in the bed, pulled the covers over my head, and fell asleep like a newborn.

Not even two hours later, my phone was ringing and fucked up the deep sleep I was in. Cheno's name was on the screen, causing me to moan loudly. I turned over, answering before it went to voicemail. "Yeah."

"What the fuck wrong wit' you, Breeze?" He screamed in my ear.

"Pipe that shit down, brah. I don't even know what you talm 'bout."

"Yo' ass can play dumb if you want to. What I tell you about throwin' yo' chest around in these streets. You should've known word was gon' get back to me."

"Cheno, let me enlighten you once again. You are not my daddy. As my big brother, I appreciate you looking out for me, but disrespect is something I won't tolerate from anybody. Bam got just what he was trying to dish out. Embarrassment. Had he walked away when I told him I didn't sell tre-fives, he would've been able to save face. Instead, his testosterone got the best of him, forcing me to show him my balls were bigger."

"Let me tell you this." Cheno paused then I heard a door slam loudly. "These niggas gon' test you every chance they get because you are beautiful, and carry more weight than most of them. They approach you wanting to fuck, not knowing you like the same shit as them. Pussy. Most of these muthafuckas don't agree with your lifestyle, but they have to respect it. You gon' cause me to catch a fuckin' case about you. All I ask is that you let me know when shit goes down so I can be prepared."

"I hear what you're saying and I'm not worried about none of that. I got you, though. Can I go back to sleep now?"

"What time are you and Sia coming to the club?"

"I'll be rolling solo. Fuck that bitch. If Sia shows up, she better stay clear of me."

"What the fuck happened? Y'all was just all over each other yesterday."

"She was sitting on my porch, questioning me about where I'd been and I ignored her ass.

When I went into the bathroom to shower, the bitch stole five hunnid from me. I told her she ended what we had when she pulled that shit. Case closed."

"Why she just didn't ask you for that lil' shit?"

"When you find out, allow her to pour her pity upon you because I wasn't trying to hear none of what she had to say.

She opened the door for me to do what I do best. Get the bitches." I laughed.

"I'll see you in a few hours, bro. I need to sleep a little bit longer before I get up and dress to impress."

"Aight, I'll holla at you later, sis. Be ready to turn up because tonight is going to be epic."

Cheno ended the call, and I rolled the fuck over pulling the covers back over my head. I was going to need all the sleep I could get because we were going to party like it was 1999.

Chapter 7

Honey

"Cheno, I am still in disbelief! I was under the impression that I was staying with you until I got on my feet."

"Now, Honey, you know damn well I've been preparing for you to touch down. There was no way I was gon' have you sleeping in my spare bedroom. I had to set you up right."

I was walking around my three-bedroom home. It was fully furnished with any and everything I needed plus more. The master bedroom was the size of the living room and kitchen of the apartment I grew up in. It had a walk-in closet that was filled from front to back with designer clothes, shoes, and purses. Cheno even installed a safe into the floor that I immediately put to use by inserting the five thousand dollars Kylie gifted until I was able to deposit it into my account. I was blessed before I set foot on the plane, but my cousin didn't short stop either. Cheno had opened an LLC account for my business and there was enough money in it to last a long time.

The adjourning bathroom had a huge jacuzzi tub on one side, and a separate shower on the other. The waterfall showerhead was my favorite amenity and I couldn't wait to indulge to test out how the water hit my body. The his and hers sinks were in the middle of the room with a big mirror with built-in lighting that luminated behind it. The setup was beautiful and very elegant. The linen closet was on the far side of the room with float away shelves for towels and other personal items.

"Honey, would you please sit down for a minute? Yo' ass making me dizzy watching you go from room to room. This yo' shit. You have nothing but time to enjoy this house."

"I'm just amazed, Cheno. I can't thank you enough," I said walking out of the bathroom. Sitting at the vanity across from my bed, I put my head in my hands. "You don't know what it feels like coming from a jail cell to a small ass room in a halfway house, to this," I said waving my hands around the room. "I never thought in my wildest dreams I would be living in a place so lavishly. Hell, I had plans to get a damn condo downtown or some shit. The business plan for Customization by Honey was something I planned to get on soon as possible, but you took care of that for me and is making serious loot too. I owe you my life, Cheno, and I promise to pay you back with interest."

"Shut up with all that. You don't owe me nothing. I told you I had yo' back and I meant every word. I love to see your face light up with every surprise I've presented to you today. We have a lot to catch up on and there is a lifetime between us to get that done. Until then, we're going to ball out tonight and have some fun. I have a few more gifts for you, but they can wait until later." Cheno paused, rubbing his hands together with a sly grin on his face.

"What are you up to, Cuz?"

"Follow me. I can't hold this one in no mo'. I gotta hit you upside the head one more time," he laughed leaving the room. "Come on, foo! I don't have all night. We got shit to do."

I scurried behind Cheno as I saw him disappear into the kitchen. As I stepped off the last step, I slowly entered the room. Running my hand along the marble countertop, I stood in the middle of the floor.

Cheno stepped aside and motioned toward the door leading to the garage. "Open the door, Honey."

There was nothing more Cheno could do for me in my mind. He'd purchased the shop, a house, and gave me all of the proceeds from the business. What else could he possibly have in store for me? My anxiety was high, and I felt like an unbalanced washer on the spin cycle as I grasped the knob. My hands were sweating profusely. Cheno laughed at my antics, and I shot a dirty look his way. Taking a deep breath, I finally opened the door. Parked in the two-car garage sat a 2023 Black Porche Cayenne SUV.

"Oh My God!" I screamed while jumping up and down. "You have really outdone yourself with this muthafucka right here! Cheno, this is too much!"

I could no longer hold back the tears that stung my eyes. A bitch was grateful for everything that was presented to me. I walked around the vehicle admiring the sleek exterior and fell in love. The twenty-inch wheels had custom rims that were outlined in hunter green. The tint on the windows were dark, but not too much that I would be fucked with by the pigs. I opened the passenger door and the first thing I saw were the custom headrests with my name engraved above the Porsche emblem in the same color as the rims. The new car scent filled my nostrils and I loved it. Stepping back, I took in the green runners that caused me to smile hard. Cheno definitely listened when I talked to him. That was my favorite color. Cruising through the streets of Chicago was something I was eager to do. Being free to do what I wanted and in style had me on cloud nine.

"This muthafucka is sick! You've taken care of everything except bringing a man into my life. You're the best cousin ever!" Hugging Cheno tightly, I couldn't stop thanking him.

"Man, gon' with all that thank you shit." He laughed. "As far as a nigga goes, I got that on lock too. I'on think you ready for him though. Big Dawg may be outta yo' league. The last nigga you had was lame as fuck in my eyes."

"Let me be the judge of that. Where he at?"

"You'll see him tonight when we hit the club. Speaking of that nigga Cheese… there's some shit I left you out of the loop about. He stopped fuckin' with you because he's with a female named Letty. I'm sorry——"

"Cheno, I knew that days ago. It's all good because both of them will see me in due time. For two muthafuckas who couldn't stand each other, they've been real lovey dovey while I was locked away behind his bullshit. Letty is the poster child of, *with friends like that, who needs enemies.*"

Cheno leaned against my whip and stared me down. "Honey, you just served ten years and I don't want to ever have to come visit you behind those walls again."

"That's something you won't ever have to worry about. Whoopin' on a bitch softly but effectively never equated to jail time. Believe me, I'm not going to kill either of them. Where are we going tonight?" I smirked, changing the subject.

"*Déjà vu* has a theme event every Monday called Big Money Mondays."

"Déjà vu. What's that?" I asked.

"It's a strip club on Clinton. It be lit in that bad boy, and I figured you could have fun while getting back into the swing of things."

I'd never been to a strip club, and I guess there was a first time for everything. There was nothing wrong with watching ass and throwing cash for one night. I was with whatever Cheno was on long as I had a grand time.

"Since you ain't never kicked it with ya boy, I have to end this day right. You may want to take a nap because we ain't leaving until they shut that shit down!"

"I'm down for whatever. It's about time I get a chance to let my hair down and get white girl wasted." We both laughed as we went back inside.

"I got some shit to take care of before we head out. I'll be back to pick you up."

"Cheno, you don't have to come back. Hit me with the location of the club and I'll be there. I'm pushing my new whip. What the fuck you thought?"

Cheno laughed while shaking his head. "You won't be able to get fucked up the way you want if you drive. I won't allow you to set yourself up like that and get pulled over for intoxication. So, yeah, I'll be back to scoop you." Cheno hugged me once more before leaving.

I headed to my bedroom to choose an outfit to wear to the strip club. I had to be one of the baddest bitches in the building and I needed to do something to my hair. The weather was beautiful, and I planned to show my ass literally for my first night out.

***

As promised, Cheno was back to pick me up at ten o'clock. He even parked his car in my garage and pulled out my Porsche to chauffeur me and Charlie to the club. I set the alarm after checking myself out in the mirror then stepped out onto the porch.

"Bitch, you betta!" Charlie screamed running toward me. "You look good as fuck! Never in a million years would I have ever thought you were packing all that under those prison clothes."

The halter bodysuit fit my frame perfectly. My boobs were sitting right and my waistline had an hourglass effect even though without it, my abs were still tight. The sheer pants with black panties underneath showcased my ass from all angles while the black stilettos accentuated my toned legs and calves. I decided on nude makeup for a natural look and bone straight hair with a part down the middle. One would believe I had a headful of extensions but that was not the case. The long tresses that flowed down my back were mine one hundred percent. Locking the door I smiled from ear to ear at Charlie's compliments, I threw my keys inside my clutch and twirled around slowly.

"I look good, huh?"

"Hell yeah! You about to have all the bitches and niggas on yo' ass tonight! The bitches that will be shaking their ass in *Déjà vu* won't be making money once you enter the building. Eyes gon' be locked on you to get some of that Honey love." Charlie laughed as she slapped Honey on her butt playfully.

"Girl, bye. I'm not gon' be paying attention to no damn body, and I won't be leaving with anyone except you and Cheno." I rolled my eyes, sashaying down the steps like a runway model.

I knew I looked like eye candy because I saw the shit for myself when I looked in the mirror. I even took a couple of pics to post on my social media profile once I was ready to get back online.

"Did y'all bring drinks?" I asked sliding into the back seat.

Cheno handed me a fifth of coconut 1800, a small bottle of pineapple juice, and a plastic cup. I poured my poison then filled the cup Charlie held out to me as well. The smell of weed eliminated the new car smell of my vehicle, but I didn't trip about it. I sat back, enjoying the ride while taking in the sights.

Yeah, bout to catch another flight
Yeah, the apple bottoms make him wanna bite
I just wanna have a good night
I just wanna have a good night
Hold up, if you don't know now you know,
If he broke then you gotta let him go
you could have anybody, eeny, miny, moe
'Cause when you a boss, you could do what you want

"Who is this?" I asked bopping to the beat.

"Coi Leray. She's Benzino's daughter."

"I don't know who that is, but this is a bop. I like the hook more than anything." I sipped my drink. "'Cause when you a boss, you could do what you want. You got that shit right! I'm about to show these muhafuckas how to boss the fuck up."

"That's what the fuck I'm talking about. It's time to live, sis."

Nodding, I agreed. Ten years was a long time to be caged like an animal. I knew firsthand how the lions, tigers, and bears felt being locked away at the zoo. The world had changed so much and I was ready to catch up.

Cheno got off the expressway downtown and traffic was ridiculous. There were so many different buildings and business that weren't there before. I didn't recognize where we were until I spotted street signs. We pulled in front of the club fifteen minutes later and Cheno exited the car. Talking to the valet attendant, he shook his hand before walking around the back of the vehicle. He opened my door then Charlie's and we both got out.

Escorting us to the entrance of the club, females were calling out to Cheno and I could see the scowl on Charlie's face. He didn't stop to address any of them as he dapped up the bouncer at the door. We were allowed in without being searched and the place was packed. There was no way we would be able to party comfortably with all these people in the building. I was having second thoughts but Cheno led us to a section that was just for us.

"We got VIP, baby! I saw how you were looking down on the little people, Honey. I do everything big around my way."

The bottle girls came right up and place bottles and food on the table. A few of Cheno's friends were already in attendance as well as Goldie, Tequila, and a few more females that were with them.

"Oooouuuu, Honey, you cute!" Tequila said standing to hug me.

"Thank you. I didn't know y'all would be here."

"Why wouldn't we be? It's your welcome home party. What better way to welcome you home than dancing, drinking, and having a good ass time?" Tequila smiled, motioning the unidentified ladies to come forward.

"This is Spanky and Tiny. Y'all, meet Honey. She's the owner of the shop I was telling y'all about."

"Nice to meet you," Tiny said. "I can't wait to work with you because it's about to be a whole vibe in the place. Not to say it's not fun now, but I believe you are going to take it to another level."

"Yeah, I have some things in mind. We will discuss that at our first meeting. Enough about business though. Your name fits you perfectly. You're so tiny; no disrespect."

Tiny stood about four feet ten inches. She was light skinned with a petite frame. Tiny had thick lips. The kind mean loved to refer as dick suckers. She was beautiful with freckles and bluish green eyes.

"I hear that shit all the time until I have to throw these guns on a bitch. Then I'm feisty, wild, and untamable." Tiny laughed.

Turning to the other woman, "You must be Spanky."

"Sharon at birth, but don't ever call me that shit. Nobody ever uses that name other than government officials and my mama. It's Spanky to everyone else."

"Duly noted."

Spanky was a little over five feet, maybe slightly taller. She was medium complected with huge breast and a big ass wagon that sat on her back. Baby girl was every man's dream when it came to a healthy woman. Spanky had all the assets and her face card wasn't lacking at all. She wore a lace front that was laid without a strand of hair out of place. I had some beautiful women on my team, and we were about to get to the bag. But first, it was time to turn up.

I decided to stick with what I was drinking in the car and poured me a cup of tequila. The others followed suit as the section filled up with more people. I didn't know any of them and that was cool because they all came to party with me. When I turned toward the entrance, I saw Breeze enter with Taz by her side. I smiled because my cousin wasn't shit like the little girl I once knew. She walked into the club as if she owned the place.

Breeze wore all black everything. The fitted shirt she wore under a short sleeved black button-down shirt that she kept open, a pair of black straight legged pants with a silver belt, and black suede dress shoes. Her silver jewelry set the outfit off perfectly. She had a silver Cuban link around her neck, a matching bracelet on her right wrist, and a silver band attached to her apple watch. The diamonds that glistened in her ears sparkled every time the light hit them. Breeze had her faux locs freshly done hanging around her face with a fresh lineup.

As Breeze and Taz made their way to the section, I peeped the envy in the eyes of many niggas who shouldn't have been lowkey hating on a female. The shit was comical because there were plenty of men shitting on them that they could direct that animosity towards. There was also a female that was staring daggers at Breeze from afar. I didn't know what that was about, but I planned to ask my cousin if she knew her.

"Hello, beautiful. You looking good," Breeze said giving me a hug.

"You know I had to step out looking my best. It's been a long time coming."

"That ass about to mesmerize these niggas up in here. You lucky we're family because shid, I would definitely shoot my shot."

"Take that shit over there somewhere, Breeze." I laughed pulling her to the railing. "You know that chick down there in the all-white? The one sitting at the bar."

"Yeah, that's Sia. Why you ask?"

"If looks could kill, you and Taz would be dead. She mugged the fuck outta y'all when you were heading up here."

"I'm not worried about her thieving ass. She was my bitch before she stole from me earlier today."

"Damn, cuz. You move on fast as hell."

"Aye, maybe Taz is where I'm supposed to be anyway. I'm about to find out though. Anyway, what you drinking?"

"Tequila is always my drink of choice. You want me to pour you some?"

"Hell nawl. I'm a Crown nigga. I see my bro knew what time it was because I see a fresh bottle on the table."

Breeze walked to get a drink and I waved at Taz. She responded by nodding her head and that's all I got out of her. It was cool with me. Eventually, she would get to know me for the woman I was and not for what she thought of me. The ladies brought over another round of drinks and we toasted to my release. As I chased the shot with some water, a group of fine ass men entered. Cheno stood smiling with his arms outstretched.

"My nigga, Jaquellis in this muthafucka!"

"Come on, Ricky, don't do me!"

Cheno's face scrunched into frown. "Aight, we even, Quell. I thought you were gon' stand me up."

I was listening to the interaction between Cheno and Mr. Chocolate from afar. So, the fine dark-skinned, bow-legged nigga with the Colgate smile was Jaquellis, huh? The way he moved smoothly through room had me feeling like a groupie. He was for sure a street dude, but don't quote me on that because it was just my assumption. The diamonds in his medallion damn near blinded me every time he moved under the lighting.

"Close your mouth," Charlie whispered in my ear.

Wiping my mouth to make sure I wasn't drooling; I couldn't believe I got caught ogling over a man who hadn't been in my presence five minutes. Hell, to be honest, he didn't even know I existed. I shook my head to focus and tuned in on the music that was blaring though the speakers. I didn't recognize the song but the beat was a hit.

I don't know how to dance but can lean
And make the ghetto bitches put their hands on their knees
Make the ghetto bitches put their hands on their knees
Make the ghetto bitches put their hands on their knees

The song must've been popular because all the ladies were out of their seats moving their asses. I was a dancer in high school, so it took nothing for me to join the crowd. One wouldn't have been able to guess I'd been in prison for years. I was truly enjoying myself and it was long overdue. The lights went from bright to dark green, but the music continued playing. I didn't know what was going on, but I went to the railing to see what was happening down below.

"It's that time! Money Makin' Mondayyyyyy is in full effect!" the DJ shouted into the mic. "We gon' start this Monday off a little different. We have a special guest in the building and I want y'all to make it rain in this muthafucka! Help me welcome Honey home!"

Hearing my name confused the fuck out of me because I didn't know what was going on. I didn't agree to do anything in that muthafuckin' club. Cheno was the person I looked around for because he had some explaining to do. when I spotted him across the room, he was walking towards me with a puzzled expression that matched my own. Charlie smiled with a gleam in her eye as she stood next to me.

"Why is he asking me to come to the stage, Cheno?"

"Hell if I know. Money Makin' Monday is for bitches to dance for these niggas for money. I didn't put you on that list, Honey. Let me go holla at this nigga."

"It was me," Charlie chimed in before Cheno could get to the stairs. "I believe my girl will get the two hundred I invested plus more. I guess you wore the perfect outfit tonight."

As bad as I wanted to cuss Charlie the fuck out, something in me wanted to actually do the shit. The inner devil inside of me whispered, *you only live once, bitch. Go get that money.* Cheno was seething as he waited for my reaction.

"I'll go up there with you—"

"Get fucked up, Charlie. I don't know why you would sign her up for that shit in the first place!"

"It's all good, Cheno. Charlie didn't do anything wrong. Plus, I'm about to do this shit."

Sashaying to the steps, I walked toward the stage as I heard Breeze and the other ladies cheering me on as they followed close behind. The DJ was geekin' up the crowd once he noticed me climbing the stage steps. I was nervous as fuck.

"Ohhhh shit! Baby girl stacked and about to put you niggas under a spell. Don't hurt 'em sexy. You about to cash out! I hope you niggas brought lots of money because there's more to come after this. I don't want no trouble when the other females get up here and y'all throwing loose change at 'em."

I laughed at what he said and that alone put me in the headspace to milk these niggas for everything in their pockets. Looking out into the crowd, my girls were standing front and center with money in hand ready to toss at me. There were catcalls and whistles coming from the men who occupied the space up close and personal. I looked up and locked eyes with the man I fucked in my mind earlier. Jaquellis stood to the side with a smirk on his face and a book bag slung over his shoulder. It was something I didn't see him with when he first entered, but he had it on his person then.

Bong. Bong. Bong.

The music started and the beat of a drum had my ass bouncing to the beat. I was naïve when it came to today's music, but again, I liked it. When I didn't move, the DJ started the track over and I was all in. Turning my back to the crowd, I allowed my ass to lead the way. The hoots and shouts were heard loudly over the music. The female artist said, *Nigga eat this ass like a plum. This pussy tight like a nun. Better chew it like its gum. Then wipe your mouth when you done.* I almost passed out because the lyrics were crazy but fit because I was eating that shit up.

I popped my ass into a split and the crowd went wild. I felt the money raining down on me and I came up with a whole provocative routine on a dime as I danced. When the beat dropped, I ate that shit up. Rolling my pussy every which way I could, I whined to the floor when the track said, *my back shots sound like bongos,* I made my ass bounce one at a time. Getting into the song, I did a back flip landing into a split, then opened my legs wide while rubbing my pussy. The stilettos I wore only made that shit look sexy as fuck.

The stage was filled with bills and I couldn't stop smiling. I worked the hell out of that song and I loved every bit of what I was doing. After twerking a little longer, I took a bow and waved at the crowd. When I looked down, Jaquellis was front and center and I didn't even notice. He had his bag unzipped, turned it upside down, and let the contents spill on the stage at my feet. He winked at me and walked away while licking his lips. My kitty pulsated in my panties and I felt a gush of wetness at my center.

"Girl, you did that!" Charlie said running up hugging me around my neck.

"I was scared as hell, but it was fun. Who the hell was that song by?"

"That was Cardi B and Megan Thee Stallion. We got to catch you up on the music. Shid, I couldn't tell you didn't know the song. You owned that muthafucka."

Breeze and Tiny were gathering my money in black garbage bags. I needed to go to the bathroom because I was sweaty and felt like a damn stripper. Seeing all the money on the stage I laughed because I didn't even have to get naked to obtain that shit. Charlie started helping with the money and I made my way to the stairs. The moment my foot came off the last step, I was grabbed by the arm roughly.

"You get out and acting like a hoe! Shaking yo' ass for money. What the fuck, Honey!"

Cheese had fire in his eyes but, why? Now he wanted to act like he was my man since I was out of prison. He had a lot to learn about me because I wasn't the same little girl he left to fend for herself in the system.

"If you don't get yo' muthafuckin hands off me." I snarled at him. "I haven't heard from you in years, now you care. Get the fuck outta my face!"

Cheno made his way through the crowd and pushed Cheese off me. Security approached and Cheno waved them off. I read his lips as he mouthed, he had it. They stood close by just in case something jumped off.

"Nigga, don't put yo' hands on her. Where yo' bitch at? That's the type of aggression you should have with her. This the wrong one for you to try manhandling. You fumbled the bag a while ago. Stand on that shit because she over you, nigga." Cheno gritted.

"Me and Honey go way back. She knows what it is. Ain't that right?" Cheese smirked.

"Nah, I don't know shit. All I know is that yo' weak ass left me at my lowest and it's a wrap after that. Like Cheno said, where's yo' bitch?" I laughed walking away, but he grabbed my arm again.

"You about to leave with me, Honey. I'm not playing with yo' ass either."

"Nigga, I got my family. She ain't going nowhere with yo' bitch ass. You better tread lightly because ya boy Tank on my hit list. He's yo' family so that means you on the choppin' block, too."

"The fuck you talking about? Whatever Tank did ain't got shit to do with me. Take that shit up with that nigga."

"Where his pussy ass at?" Cheno barked.

92

"Find him." Cheese laughed. "I'm not a fuckin' snitch. Why would I lead you to my blood? That's not how this shit works. Take that how you want, playa."

"Bet. When I find him, he's good as dead. Get ya black suit out, you gon' need it."

"Is that a threat?"

"Nah, that's a muthafuckin' promise," Cheno said with conviction.

Cheese nodded while grabbing my hand. "Come on, Honey."

I snatched away and out of my peripheral I saw Letty storming in our direction. Not only was this nigga demanding I leave with him, but he had his bitch in tow. What the hell did Cheese expect me to do, ride out with the both of them? I think the fuck not! I waited until Letty was standing ten toes down besides Cheese before I let loose on her ass.

"Bitch, you got a lot of nerve showing yo' face around me!"

Letty stumbled from the blow I delivered to her right eye. She didn't fall because of the grip I had on the front of her dress. Drawing back to clock her ass again, I was swept off my feet. The anger inside me came out full force as I struggled to get away from whomever interrupted the beat down I had in store for Letty.

"Nah, ma. You not going out like that. The nigga ain't worth the attention you're giving him." Jaquellis whispered in my ear, but his tone was firm.

I stopped struggling and allowed him to carry me out the side door. The way he held me along with the scent of his cologne calmed me down immediately. He didn't put me on down until we got outside. Standing over six feet, Jaquellis looked at me with so much sincerity. The way he studied my face as if he wanted to reach out and touch me sent a shiver down my spine. I hated that anybody had to witness me in the element I was in when Letty made her presence known.

"You too cute to be cutting up like that in public. Never allow a nigga take you out of character. It's obvious he doesn't care about you. Once you allow a man to play in your face, he gon' keep doing that shit." Jaquellis paused to see if I was going to respond, but I didn't so he continued.

"I've heard so much about you from Cheno. You've had it rough, baby girl, and it's gonna take a minute for you to bounce back. Leave that nigga in the past because nothing good can come from that situation. I can tell you and ole girl got some type of history."

Nodding I took a deep breath. "Yeah, we do. Letty was my best friend back in the day. To learn that she is with the man I thought I loved pissed me off because as far as I knew, she couldn't stand his ass. Now, they've been together eight muthafcukin' years and he said fuck me while I was serving time for his shit! Hell yeah, I tried to tear her head off her neck."

"And that's reason enough right there for you to walk away from all of the negativity. All I can say is, concentrate on the positive, Honey. You are strong and I don't want you to get caught up in no bullshit."

Jaquellis stared at me with pure admiration and I could feel my face heating up. Turning slightly away from him, Jaquellis used his finger to bring my attention back his way. I forgot all about the altercation I was involved in when he brought me in for a hug.

"You look better in person. The pictures I've seen doesn't do you any justice."

Stepping out of his embrace, I glared at him quizzingly because I was clueless as to how he'd seen pictures of me. I knew nothing about this man and here he was saying he'd been basically admiring me through images. My curiosity got the best of me. I had questions that needed answers.

"Where did you see pictures of me?"

He chortled. "Cheno has you on display in his crib. For a minute I thought you were his woman until meeting Charlie.

When he revealed you were his cousin, I was determined to meet you."

"Why? Do you know where I've been for years?"

"Of course, I know where you were, and why wouldn't a real man want to meet such a beautiful woman? You are the reason I'm here. I couldn't pass up the opportunity to get to know you inside out. The world isn't the way you remember them. I know your temper is set to go off like a M-80 and I won't watch you destroy your life before you get the chance to live again."

Cheno had to have told this man my back story and it didn't sit well with me. I wasn't embarrassed about where I'd been, but I didn't want the entire world to be able to talk about what I had been through either. My cousin and I was going to have a conversation soon enough.

"Listen, I appreciate you wanting to be there for me. I'm very capable of easing back into this thing called life on my own. It's gonna be a hard journey trying to find out who I am. The way you are gazing at me, I don't want to sound conceited, but I think you may want more than I can give."

"All I want at this time is to get to know you, Honey. Whatever happens during that process is all up to you. We can build a friendship and start there. What do you say?"

Before I could answer, the door opened behind Jaquellis and Cheese emerged with a scowl on his face. I rolled my eyes with a heavy sigh. Cheese was doing the most for someone who abandoned me, been in a relationship with a former friend, and I needed him to stand on the decision he made.

"Let me holla at you." Cheese grabbed me aggressively by the arm while trying to lead me away from Jaquellis. Once again, I snatched away and stepped back.

"Aye, man. Why you keep handling her like you here pimp or some shit?"

"I don't know who you is, homie, but this my bitch!" Cheese snarled at Jaquellis with a menacing stare. "I'd advise you to find somebody else's business to attend to, nigga."

Yo' bitch? Cheese—"

"What did we just talk about, Honey?" Jaquellis asked, cutting me off. He pulled me behind him without taking his eyes off Cheese. "Check it. Her name is Honey as you already know. Not bitch. Address her as such or we gon' have problems."

"Again, who the fuck is you to correct me?"

"I'm about to be your worst nightmare, nigga. You got a lot of nerve demanding this woman's attention after you left her high and dry in the prison system. On top of that, you got a bitch inside that building," Jaquellis snapped, pointing his thumb behind him, "while you out here in my woman's face."

I was confused as hell because at what point did I agree to be this man's woman? Listening to the way he stood up to Cheese behind me made my stomach flutter. That shit went away quickly and, in an instant, it felt like I had to shit when Cheese's voice bellowed.

"Nigga, I'll kill over mine!" Cheese mugged. "That bitch will forever belong to me!"

In a millisecond, Jaquellis punched Cheese one time and he hit the ground with a thud. His loud snores could be heard clearly. The fire in Jaquellis eyes were something I'd never seen before. It was as if he'd morphed into Satan instantaneously. He snatched his tool from his waistband and aimed it at Cheese.

"No! He's not worth it, remember? Let's just go," I pled, pulling him by the arm.

Jaquellis led me to his car with his pistol still in his hand. He opened the passenger door for me and I got in nervously. I studied his every move after he closed me in and walked around the car. When he got in, he was on his phone.

"Cheno, I got Honey with me. That nigga Cheese is laid out on the side of the building. He's gonna be a problem so keep ya eyes on the swivel." I couldn't hear what my cousin said on the other end, so I sat quietly. Jaquellis looked over at me then stated, "We'll be at her crib. I'll see you when you pull up."

Chapter 8

Letty

Honey had me all the way fucked up. She had no reason to jump on me in front of all those people in the club. Then again, she had every right because Cheese had been caressing my walls for the past eight years. It wasn't my fault her stupid ass took a charge that cost her ten years of her life. There was no way in hell I would do some shit like that for a nigga.

Me and Honey were best of friends during high school. We did everything together and I was her shoulder to cry on whenever James tried to make a move on her. He would do all types of weird shit while her mother was at work. Honey would escape to my house. It was me who asked my mother if she could spend the night so she wouldn't be alone with his pedophile ass. All that changed when she met Cheese.

We had gone from hanging out all day, every day to barely. Word got around about James getting killed and I asked Honey if she knew anything about it. Honey's answer was always the same; no. I didn't believe her. Pam, her mother, wouldn't have put her out otherwise. Hell, she thought Honey was behind the murder too. That's why she hadn't gone to one visit while her daughter was locked up.

Cheese saved Honey and it went to her head. In my opinion, Honey thought she was better than me and our friendship went from sugar to shit. She went from a girl who had the bare minimum to having everything she ever wanted.

Except her man to herself. Every time I saw Cheese with a bitch, I would let Honey know. We were fighting bitches daily behind that nigga. He was cheating with anything with a pussy. It didn't matter if the female was fat, skinny, tall, short, or ugly than a muthafucka. If she could open her legs, Cheese would crawl between them. I took her to see the shit with her own eyes and Honey still didn't leave him. After a while she told me to mind my business and I did just that.

I didn't like the way Cheese treated Honey, but I lowkey wanted him myself. Playing the role of hating his guts was hard and I pulled it off in her presence. But when she got knocked, I was on that nigga like flies on shit. Honey was gone a month before I had Cheese's dick down my throat. I was known as being a certified head doctor and it took one take to have that muthafucka's toes curling and his babies coating my tongue.

As I washed the makeup from my face, I became mad all over again for what happened at the club. Cheese lied and told me a group of niggas tried to rob him outside the club but I knew better. He went out chasing Honey's funky ass and probably got handled by the nigga that carried her out after she assaulted me. Cheese shut me up when I questioned him in the car but that shit wouldn't happen a second time. Wasn't nobody getting no sleep until he told me why he thought it was okay to approach the hoe. Taking a deep breath, I walked into the bedroom we share and noticed him scrolling through his phone.

"You ready to talk now?" I asked calmly.

"Ain't shit to talk about, Letty." Cheese didn't bother to look up from his phone.

"Oh, that's a lie and you know it. Honey is the shit I want to talk about. You ain't seen nor talked to the bitch in eight years but you decided to manhandle her at the club as if she's still your woman. Explain that shit so I'll understand."

Cheese tossed his phone onto the bed and mugged me. The way his jaw twitched let me know he was pissed. I didn't give a fuck because his disrespectful ass had me seeing red too. I was prepared to stand toe to toe with him like we were two pit bulls in a dog fight.

"I don't have to explain nothing to you. I will tell you this though, Honey and I have history and yo' ass know how far back that goes. She will always be a factor in my life whether you like it or not. The only reason I stopped communicating with her while she was locked up was because I had established something with you."

"Nigga, the mission was and still is accomplished! Just because her jailbird ass is back on the streets don't mean you about to pick that shit up where y'all left off." I walked around the bed until I was standing in front of him. "What ain't about to happen is you sneaking around with the hoe. My name ain't Honey and I'm not competing with her!"

Cheese laughed while shaking his head. "Letty, you ain't never been in Honey's league. Competing? If that's the case, you already lost. No woman has ever come before her."

"The lies you tell, nigga. I ain't never had to fuck a bitch up behind you. Honey was fighting until her knuckles bled trying to keep them hoes off yo' dick!" I smirked at his ass.

"See, that's where you're wrong. The only reason she was throwing hands in the streets is because you were bringing her to the catfight. Letty, you don't think I know what you was on back then? I could've fucked you right under Honey's nose and she wouldn't have found out about it. Why? Yo' thirsty ass wasn't gon' tell on ya'self. Plus, I didn't want to bring that type of hurt into her life. As far as you fighting other bitches, what you don't know won't hurt you. Stay in yo' lane, Letty."

"What the fuck that supposed to mean?"

"You don't want to know that truth, trust me. But use your imagination and hurt yo damn self. In the meantime, I need to go handle some business. When I return, this shit better be a thing of the past or we are done."

Cheese walked out before I could even say anything in return. The bullshit was starting and I was determined to keep Honey's gullible ass out of the equation. Once I heard Cheese's car revved out of the driveway, I dialed up my sisters on facetime. Shalonda and Shaveen both answered the call in the dark because it was damn near three in the morning.

"What the fuck did Cheese do?" Shaveen asked sleepily.

"He is sniffing up Honey's ass!"

"Honey? I thought she was locked up," Shalonda said turning on the light.

"Turn that damn light off, Shalonda! I have to get up in a few hours."

"Shut up, Aiden. My sister needs me," she barked back getting out of the bed naked as the day she was born. "I don't say shit when your piss poor of a brother calls all times of the night and you're talking loud as fuck!"

Shalonda slammed the door and Aiden could be heard screaming something in the background but she ignored him like she always did. Shaveen was laughing loud as hell on the other end of the phone because she loved when our sister punked her boyfriend. Flopping on the sofa in her living room, Shalonda covered her chest with a crochet throw.

"When is that man going to grow some balls?" Shaveen asked.

"Never. His ass knows better. Aiden better play that tough shit with his unseasoned ass mammy. Every day I think about going out to find me a big dick nigga. His ass is lucky his pockets long as fuck or he would be out of this muthafucka."

"That's his house though," Shaveen laughed.

"Shut up, Veen! Anyway, like I was saying, I thought Honey was in prison."

"She's out."

I told them what happened at the club and the two of them was quiet as church during prayer. I had to look down at the phone to make sure they were still there. Shaveen had turned the light on in her room and was sitting straight up.

"What did you expect, Letty? You broke the girl code when you started fucking behind her."

"Shalonda, you worried about the wrong shit!" Shaveen snarled. "Did you not hear our sister say the bitch snaked her? We don't play those types of games. Honey has to get handled."

"That's what the fuck I'm talking about! I knew my sisters would have my back," I exclaimed with a smile.

"No, you have Shaveen. I'm too grown for all that fighting shit and I have wayyyyy too much to lose. All I can say is this, don't go to jail behind a nigga that's going to do what he wants regardless."

It didn't surprise me that Shalonda wasn't down with beating the fuck out of Honey. She had an image to uphold with Aiden and his uppity ass family. I hated the fact that she went to the other side of the tracks because she only let her ghetto side out in front of Aiden's ass. Other than that, she acted like the black Mary Poppins when around his people. Eyes were always on her waiting for her to fuck up.

With Aiden's father being a successful surgeon, and his mother a celebrity real estate agent, they were always worried about any kind of slander. Neither was pleased with their son's choice of woman, but they respected it as far as we could see. I believed they talked shit about Shalonda behind closed doors. They were smart enough to keep it amongst themselves because our family would destroy them publicly.

"Just be quiet, sis. If push came to shove, I know you gon' ride. You can take the bitch out the hood, but the hood will always be in the bitch. Remember, we are one and the same. Ain't no fooling me," Shaveen rolled her eyes. "Letty, when you ready let me know and we're gonna beat that hoe the fuck up. Until then, I'm going to bed because yo' sister just blew the shit out of me."

"Aight. I have to find out where that bitch laying her head. It may be a minute because she just got out. I know for a fact her mama ain't fucking with her so finding out anything may be hard."

"Check that bitch social media. You can find anything on that shit. Keep me posted. Goodnight, and Shalonda, find yo' blackness. I don't recognize you, boo."

"Fuck you."

Shalonda hung up, making Shaveen laugh before hanging up. Knowing at least one of my sisters was riding with me, I got under the covers and started scrolling social media. Allowing Honey to roam around thinking everything was sweet was a no go. I had to find out where she was because she started a war when she put hands on me. I just hope she was ready when I pulled up on her.

***

The sun beamed into the window as my alarm blared from my phone. I silenced the device and snuggled back under the covers. I didn't want to get up to get ready for work, but I knew I had to. So many of my friends thought it was crazy that I worked a job when I had a man like Cheese. See, that was where I differed from a lot of the bird brains in the hood. There was no way I would sit around waiting for a nigga to give me anything. Don't get me wrong, every dime Cheese gave me, a percentage went into my savings. My mama didn't raise a dummy. I would be good with or without Cheese. I may be a manager at the Hyatt Regency, but I'd been saving for eight years and I was going to be just fine.

Reaching out to hug my man, I came up empty. My hand caressed the coolness of his side of the bed. The muthafucka didn't have the decency to come back in the house after the shit he'd said the night before. Cheese was rude as fuck and I went to sleep to put that shit behind me. Then he had the nerve to stay out all night.

103

If I found out he was with that bitch, Honey, I was going to shoot both of them with some hot shit. Instead of lying around angry, I got up and made my way to the bathroom to take care of my hygiene. A slight headache was trying its best to cripple me and I had to get ahead of it. I shook two Advil tablets in my hand, swallowing them with a small Dixie cup of water. In a matter of time, I would feel a lot better.

I jumped into the shower and washed every crevice of my body. The hot water woke me up fully and I was lost in the moment. It seemed as if I was in the shower for a long period of time but it was barely ten minutes. A cool gust of air hit my back and I wiped water from my face frantically. My heart was beating erratically in my chest. The thought of someone stabbing me while I washed my ass terrified the fuck out of me.

"My bad, ma. I didn't mean to scare you," Cheese apologized as he raised his leg to get in the shower with me.

Being frightened was a thing of the past when I remembered his dick wasn't poking me in my back when I woke up. I had never rinsed my body so fast in life, but I handled that shit in record time. Cheese tried to kiss the back of my neck and I swerved his ass then exited the shower.

"What's yo' problem?"

"You! How dare you come in here trying to butter up to me after talking shit and being out all night. A smart man would've cleaned his dick before leaving the bitch."

"Letty, there you go in your feelings again," Cheese said with a frown. "I've been here all night. Yo' ass was all over the bed so I slept in the other room."

"Stop lying! You was not here!"

I left the bathroom, dried my body and got dressed for work. The black pantsuit I picked out the night before fit my body like a glove. As I slipped my feet into my black heeled pumps, Cheese entered the bathroom.

"Are you gon' sit down and talk to me?"

"Nope. Did you want to talk last night?" I asked applying a light coat of lip gloss. "Don't start something you wouldn't want me to finish, Cheese. Do you, though."

"I told you I was in this muthafucka! When you assume, you make an ass out of yourself, Letty. There ain't been another female in years. Maybe I should go out and do just what you accusing me of."

I swung around quick as hell after he said that shit. "You insinuated that shit already. Even downed me while lusting over that bitch Honey. If going back in time is what you want to do, make that shit happen. The way you reacted to my question about the way you acted at the club, you took that shit all the way into left field. I'm not stupid by a long shot. Dumb is something I would never be and sitting back watching you frolic around like a blind mouse won't happen either. Once you fuck outside of me, I'm gon' ride the nearest dick or two myself."

Cheese took a few gigantic steps and was across the room in no time flat. His hand clutched my throat before I knew what was transpiring. The element of surprise caused me to stop breathing momentarily.

"That's the wrong shit you can say to a nigga like me. I will kill yo' ass in this muhfucka! I don't give a fuck if twenty bitches was taking turns sucking my dick, you on the other hand don't have the same satisfaction. That shit is grounds for you to get fucked up! I'm the only nigga you would ever entertain! Try it if you want to."

Cheese had fire in his eyes that I'd never seen in all the years of being with him. My inner self yelled, *"You pushed him too far! Why did you say that?"* I couldn't respond because the words in my mind were caught in my throat too. He pushed me away from him and stormed to the closet.

"Go the fuck to work before I swell yo' ass up."

I hurried up and grabbed my phone, purse, and keys before making a beeline out of the house. I was shaking like a hoe on Cicero as I pushed the start button on my Lexus truck. Sitting quietly, I ran back everything from last night to present time and I was pissed off all over again. Cheese threw bitches in my face as if it was a privilege to be with his ass. The disrespectful shit he let fall from his mouth wasn't a mistake because he did it twice with no remorse.

Knowing that Cheese thought more highly of Honey than he did me only heightened my anger. I knew where I stood with him. There was no way in hell I was going to put my all into a muthafucka who still had feelings for someone he left to hang themselves for years. Honey would be stupid to give him another chance. I wasn't going back on what I said to him. Two could play that game and Cheese was going to need a defibrillator when I matched his energy.

Chapter 9

Cheese

The things I'd said to Letty was something I would've said back in the day. What I said about fucking around with her while with Honey wasn't a lie. Letty was the reason Honey knew what I was doing in the street, but I hadn't been with another woman since being with her. Seeing Honey in the club did something to me because I wasn't aware of her being out of prison. She should've gotten in touch with me the moment she stepped foot back in Chicago.

Honey had every right to be upset about me moving on without her. I made a vow that I would ride out the sentence with her, but I wasn't expecting the law to throw ten years at her the way they had done. I visited often while she was in the County then she was shipped to a prison in Washington. From that point, I kept money on her books until I made a commitment to Letty. Taking care of Honey was something she insisted stopped immediately once she found out what I was doing. Letty was my girl so honoring her wishes was something I decided to do as her man.

Everything was good with us until the night before. I would be the first to admit that I did the most when I approached Honey. In my mind, she belonged to me no matter what I had going on in my life. Honey owed me for killing her stepfather and teaching her everything she knew about the street life. If it wasn't for me, she would have been eating out of garbage cans and sleeping on park benches because her mama didn't give a fuck about her ass. I was the only nigga she'd ever slept with so her pussy was trained to get wet for one dick; and that was mine.

When the nigga Cheno pushed me away from Honey, I wanted to beat his ass. Instead, I remained calm because Honey wasn't interested in his ass intimately. Cheno let it be known that she was his family and that shit threw me for a loop. Where the fuck was her *family* when she needed them years prior? That shit went out the window when Cheno started talking about my cousin Tank hitting up his spot. He was coming for the wrong muthafucka with that shit because I didn't have a reason to clam his pockets up.

I had everything I needed on the westside and robbing a muthafucka was not my forte. Tank on the other hand would steal from a dead nigga lying in the middle of the street. Just because he was my family didn't mean I condoned how he made his money. For Cheno to come at me with the bullshit meant he expected me to pay for something I had nothing to do with. He put his foot in his mouth when he thought I was going to give my family up like a bitch. I meant what I said when I told his punk ass to find Tank. The threats he threw out didn't rattle me but I'd heard how Cheno operated in the streets. We'd never had any problems until Tank decided to stick his hand in the cookie jar.

Letty was at my neck the moment we got in the car at the club because she found me sitting on the curb with my head in my hand. I told her some niggas tried to rob me instead of telling her what really took place. Honey and that nigga she was with was going to see me. No bitch had ever left me. I did the letting go and Honey knew that shit. Whoever the nigga was proclaimed he was her man but the confusion on her face told me he was lying. It didn't matter though because Honey knew what time it was.

I ignored her all the way to the home we shared. Letty pushed me to the limit as she kept questioning me. Every other word that came out of her mouth had Honey dripping from it. Hearing that name only pissed me off. I gave her more than enough chances to leave the shit alone and she kept forcing my hand. I gave her the answers she was seeking and Letty couldn't blame anyone but herself.

Leaving the house, I thought about going on the hunt for Honey but I didn't know where the fuck to start. Had I not been with Letty, her crib would've been the first place to look. Seeming that Honey whooped her ass for betraying her, protecting Letty was something I was gonna have to do too. In the meantime, I floored my Benz at a high rate of speed to find Tank. His ass was forever doing shit that came back to me off the strength of him being my cousin. The shit wasn't going to fly with Cheno. He wasn't like the other niggas out on the street. Tank had bit off more than he could chew and had me smack dab in the middle.

I turned on to Leamington Avenue ten minutes after I started my whip. What would've taken thirty minutes was no time the way I was driving in the wee hours of the morning. My aunt Verna's house was in the middle of the block and surprisingly there was a park not too far away. Exiting my vehicle, I made my way down the street and up the worn steps. The block was quieter than a cemetary. I made sure of that because no one was allowed to hang out or serve any type of drug anywhere near my family.

Unlocking the door, I walked in silently and made my way to the back of the house. The room Tank usually slept in was empty. Dirty clothes littered the floor, shoes were all over the place, and the bed was unmade. Tank was a slob in every way. From his appearance to his lifestyle, he was just messy. As I looked round all I could do was shake my head. The room was disgusting compared to the rest of the house. The only thing that sat out was the big screen television and the gaming system I'd gifted his ass a few years prior.

"LaDarrius, is that you?" My Aunt Verna asked using my government name as she appeared from the darkness.

"Yeah. I was looking for Tank, have you seen him?"

"He came by earlier and said he was going out of town for a few days. Tank left three thousand dollars saying that was for the bills he owed. What did he do?"

I didn't want to tell my aunt that her son was a dead man walking, but I couldn't leave her in the dark. Aunt Verna knew Tank wasn't shit. She'd said it every day since he was in high school and she was right.

"Tank stole a lot of money from somebody and they threatened to kill him. If you talk to him, make sure he never steps foot back in Chicago. Then advise him to call me. I'm his only way out of this bullshit."

"Watch yo' mouth in my house, LaDarrius. I've told you time and time again to leave that narcotic alone. But nooooo, you want to make that fast money and, in the process, killing your own people."

I laughed lowly to stop myself from disrespecting my mama's sister. It didn't work out that way though. "The only time you have a problem with the money I make is when yo' son gets hemmed up in some shit. I don't know how many times I have to tell you; Tank don't sell drugs! The shit he does in the street is a disgrace to the shit I do. He robs niggas for a living and this time he stole from the wrong muthafucka. Tank is too irresponsible to be on my payroll. If he was willing to clean up his act, I wouldn't hesitate to put him on. His pockets would always be laced. That can't happen now because he done fucked up for the last time. My name is wrapped up in his bullshit causing me to be in a war I had nothing to do with."

"Somebody is going to kill my baby?" she cried out with tears streaming down her face.

"Tell Tank to holla at me, auntie," I said ignoring her question. "You have mothing to worry about because nobody knows you're his mother. Shit like this is the reason I kept this block clean for years. You can thank me later. For now, I gotta get back home. Make sure Tank hit my line." I walked *out of the room with my aunt on my heels. With hand on the doorknob, my aunts voice burned my ears.*

"We can go to the police and they can go arrest whoever is after my child."

I turned around faster than light and grabbed her by the shoulders. "Leave the police out of this shit! If you do that, yo' ass going to jail right along with everybody else because you accepted three thousand dollars from yo' sticky fingered ass son! Do as I asked and let me handle this shit my way!"

Leaving my aunt where she stood, I slammed the door, muffling her cries. There was no way I could think with her ass making every damn excuse for Tank without seeing the fuck up that he truly was. Aunt Verna spent countless nights worried for the safety of her only child and his fat ass still found a way to sink deeper into manure. The entire way home I tried to figure out what I knew about Cheno. I came up blank. I called one of my people to dig into his life with a fine-toothed come and get back with me.

The thoughts of all I'd endured the night before ran through my mind as well as what transpired with Letty when I woke up. Shit was falling apart rapidly and I didn't like that at all. From business to my relationship, things were running smoothly until Honey resurfaced.

I sat on the edge of the bed smoking a blunt as I recalled how I almost beat the hell out of my lady. Letty was loyal to me and loved me unconditionally and I was ready to throw all that away for somebody I had groomed to fall in love with me. Honey needed me and that was something that made my dick extra hard. She didn't have a job so that meant I was her source of income. With her just getting out of jail, Honey didn't have shit to fall back on. In my mind, she needed me to get her back on her feet. In due time, she would find a way to contact me asking for daddy's help.

***

With a jerk chicken dinner on the passenger seat, I made my way downtown. Letty didn't deserve what I'd done to her and I owed her an apology. As I pulled up to her job, I doubled parked and got out. When I stepped into the lobby of the hotel, Letty was grinning from ear to ear in a muthafucka's face. *Once you fuck outside of me, I'm gon' ride the nearest dick or two myself.* Letty's words echoed in my ears causing me to get angry again. I took a few deep breaths and calmly walked up to the desk.

"Let me take you to lunch, beautiful. No strings attached," the well-dressed man said with a smile.

Letty's eyes ballooned out of her head when she spotted me. The smile dropped from her face in a flash and she tried to get back to business as she typed away on the keyboard. The dude stood with a broad grin as he waited for Letty to respond to his invitation for lunch. Meanwhile, I waited patiently to see how she would handle the problem at hand. The way her hands were shaking, I could tell she didn't know what was bound to happen to her or his ass for that matter. Letty finally looked up from the computer and handed the guest a room key.

"You are all set, Mr. O'Brien. If there's anything I can help you with just call down and we will be glad to assist you."

"That's good to know. Now, about lunch…"

"She already has lunch plans, brah. Take yo' key and find you something safe to do," I spat. My patience was thinner than a muthafucka with thrombocytopenia, the medical term for thin blood.

"LaDarrius——"

I turned my attention to her and she knew right away to shut the fuck up. Ol' boy peeped the drill and retrieved his card before grabbing his bags to leave. I watched his every move until he rounded the corner towards the elevators and wished the muthafucka would look back at my woman. The assault I put on his ass would've definitely had me spending a day in lockup.

"That was not even necessary, Cheese. This is my place of employment in case you have forgotten."

Leaning on the counter until I was nose to nose with her smart mouthed ass, I whispered so only she could hear. "Your job is to get these punk ass muthafuckas a room. Not smiling and contemplating going to fucking lunch with another man!" I sneered. "The shit you let come out yo' mouth this morning is starting to make sense. You already had plans to fuck somebody else and used the Honey situation to get the ball rolling. Well, I'm here to let you know, I will hurt you in the process. Be yo' ass home soon as you get off."

I left Letty's ass right there and exited the building before I was forced to embarrass her. She was calling my name repeatedly, but I ignored that shit because I didn't have anything to say after that. Approaching my whip, my phone rang in my pocket. It was Letty and I silenced the call, jumped behind the wheel, and pulled off. I drove through the downtown traffic until I merged onto the expressway heading westbound.

It was time for me to get back to the money. I hit up my people at all my spots to inform them to have my bread ready for pickup. The first stop I made was to Madison and Albany to meet up with Main. He was standing in wait on the porch when I pulled up. Main grabbed the duffle bag and descended the steps while checking his surroundings.

"What up, Cheese?" He asked, closing the passenger door.

"Shid, too much shit." I blazed up and blew the smoke through my nose. "Tank ass done hit up that nigga Cheno's spot. The muthafucka approached me in the club talking about since Tank is my family, my head is on the chopping block too."

"You did his ass in, right?"

"Nah, I waved that shit off because I was trying to get Honey out of there acting like a hoe."

Main turned in the seat facing me with a perplexed look on his face. "Honey? When the fuck she get out? Fuck that, where the hell was Letty while all this was going on?"

Shaking my head, I took another pull from my blunt because I knew Main was about to lay in on my ass for what took place. He knew I was going to Déjà vu to celebrate Letty's birthday and he couldn't come out with us. It had been a minute since any of us had gone to have a good time at a club.

"Come on nigga, tell me what happened!"

"I confronted Honey after she participated in that Money Monday shit. Seeing her shaking her ass on the stage pissed me off for one. Then, she didn't even reach out to me about her release. I cuffed her ass up by the arm and told her lets go. She refused. Then that nigga Cheno popped up talking about he had her. Did you know they were related?"

"Nigga, all I know is that she lived with her mother and I took part in killing the muthafucka who was trying to take advantage of her. Honey is what I know about. Hell, where the fuck was his ass when she needed him?"

"My thoughts exactly. Find out anything you can on Cheno. I need to know everything. Anyway, Letty came over and Honey beat her ass. Some nigga I've never seen carried Honey out of the club and drove off with her."

I didn't tell Main the whole truth because that shit was embarrassing and I had an image to uphold. The mystery man would get what he deserved soon as I identified his ass. Since he called Honey his woman, finding her would lead me to his ass.

"I see we have other business to deal with out in these streets. We haven't put in work in a minute and I'm ready for whatever. Just say the word and I'll gear the fuck up. As far as Cheno, I will do my homework on him then get back to you with my findings. Until then, stay away from Honey!

Cheese, you and Letty been going strong for years. Don't go back in time trying to get Honey back. Nothing good is going to come from that, my nigga."

"She owes me!"

"Honey don't owe you shit! If anything, yo' ass owes her for leaving her high and dry while you were out here fuckin' on her best friend! Like I said, leave that shit alone and take yo' frustrations out on Tank's bum ass," Main huffed. "Man, all your money is there. I'm out. Hit me if you need me. I'm telling you now, Cheese, don't call me with no bullshit."

Main exited my whip and slammed the door. There wasn't nothing left for me to do at that stop so I headed to my next destination. It took about an hour and a half for me to make all my pickups. Stopping to grab something to eat, I went home to count my money. When I walked into my house from the garage, my phone rang. Once again it was Letty and I sent her to the voicemail for the fourth time since leaving her job. I had more important shit to worry about. Listening to Letty beg and plead wasn't one of them.

Chapter 10

Honey

"What a welcome home for me."

As I rolled out of bed, I laughed at the night I'd had. It wasn't all bad once I arrived home. Jaquellis was heated from his confrontation with Cheese and he wanted to go back out to handle him accordingly. It took a while for me to talk him down along with a few shots of Remy. Cheno, Charlie, Breeze, and Taz joined us a little while later and the celebration continued.

I learned a lot about the man who saved me from catching another case so soon after coming home. Jaquellis was born and raised in Dallas, Texas where he still resided. He was the second oldest of four with two sisters and a brother. Jaquellis and his siblings made sure their mother wanted for nothing since they were all she had since the separation from their father. Hydea, his youngest sister was nineteen and attended Texas A&M University. She adored her big brother so much. Honey had the opportunity of seeing her on Facetime when Hydea called to make sure Jaquellis was okay here in Chicago.

Cheno and Jaquellis were partners in the drug game. While Cheno had things on lock in Chicago, Jaquellis did his thing in Dallas. He also owned a few gas stations, car washes, and two tattoo parlors called Quell's Inkspirations. I loved his drive and the determination to succeed in everything he did in life.

The way the two of us laughed and joked around was music to my ears. Jaquellis spoke on the idea of us being together but I stuck to my guns. It wasn't the time for me to jump into a relationship. He agreed to be friends and that was all I asked. The sun slowly rose, letting us know we had partied all night long. I told everyone to find a spot to rest because I was going to bed. In no time flat, I was sleeping like a baby.

It was well past one in the afternoon when I went into the bathroom to handle my hygiene. After showering, I threw on a pair of lounge pants, a belly top, and my slippers, then headed out of the bedroom to check on everybody. I walked to the guest bedroom down the hall from mine and knocked lightly.

"Come in."

Doing as told, I pushed the door open slowly and peeked my head in. Breeze and Taz were cuddled up like lovebirds looking real cute together. With low eyes, Breeze licked her lips while caressing Taz's arm.

"What up, Lala Ali," Breeze laughed. "Man, you were beating that bitch ass like she was on a slave plantation. What's the deal with that? I wasn't gonna be the one to bring the vibe down by asking last night."

"Hold that thought. Hello, Taz. How are you?" I asked.

She threw her arm up and snuggled deeper under the covers. I was always raised to speak when present in someone's home. The way Taz dismissed me was mad disrespectful and I was about to go in on her ass, but Breeze beat me to the punch.

"How the fuck you laying half naked in my cousin's house, in her bed, and yo' ass can't speak. Who raised yo' disrespectful ass?" Breeze snapped. "Get up and address her correctly, Taz." She did what she was told when she realized Breeze was visibly upset.

"Hey, Honey," Taz said nonchalantly.

Breeze pushed her away and got up from the bed. The boxers she wore hugged her thighs as she adjusted the sports bra she wore. Throwing on a pair of joggers and a tank, she then slipped her feet into her slides. I didn't know where she got clothes from because staying the night at my house was not in the plans the night before. Taz watched Breeze's every move and so did I because the way she was breathing, I thought she was going to jump all over Taz and beat her face in.

"Be dressed when I come back. Until you learn home training, you won't be accompanying me here anymore. Check your attitude at the door when you come to work too. It will be your fault if you say something out of the way and Honey fires your ass. I won't fight for you to stay employed."

"Honey, I apologize..."

"Girl shut the fuck up! Come on, Honey." Breeze stormed out of the room and I stayed where I stood.

"Taz, I don't know you, and you damn sure don't know me. Whatever animosity you have towards me, I hope it's not based on someone else's perception of me. I would advise you to get to know me yourself because to judge me, you have to know me. Tighten up, baby girl. I return the same energy that is given. You better ask Charlie about me. I promise, this is not what you want."

Leaving the room, I closed the door behind me and went to find my cousin to see if she had calmed down. Breeze was in the kitchen rummaging through my refrigerator. She had lettuce, tomatoes, cheese, and bread on the counter. She closed the fridge with her hip and placed the freshly cut turkey with the other items. Noticing I had joined her, Breeze took a deep breath.

"Honey, I'm sorry about that. I don't know what Taz's problem is, but I have an idea." '

"Fill me in because I'm clueless," I said dragging a barstool close to where she was working.

"Taz and Charlie have been closer than thieves from the moment she started working at the shop. She may feel you are going to interfere with the bond the two of them have established. On top of that, Taz been holding the shop down as Charlie's right hand and with you being introduced as the owner, that threatens her."

"That's stupid. She can still do all the things she's been doing. I'll be there to make sure shit is done correctly and the way I want," I said waving off the explanation she gave. The shit was childish and I wasn't going to feed into it any longer. "Taz will be aight. Anyway, what you cooking?"

"Paninis and home fries." Breeze continued cutting up the vegetables and turned the sandwich maker on to heat up. "So, tell me, who the broad was you beat up last night?"

"Oh, that was Letty, my former best friend and the bitch that's fucking the nigga I took the charge for."

"Hold up. That hoe smiled in your face and went behind you with his ass?"

"Yup. The funny thing is, they argued all the time as if they couldn't stand each other. I never got the vibe that they were fuckin' around ever," I said stealing a slice of tomato from the cutting board. "When I saw the post Cheese put up praising that bitch not knowing I was back on the street, it was already in my mind to whoop her ass on sight. I didn't beat her ass the way I wanted but I will see her again."

Breeze laughed. "I feel you on that and I hope I'm there when the shit goes down. I would hate for the bitch and her homies to catch you alone. Then all hell gon' break loose. Hell, if Quell hadn't carried you out of that muthafucka, Letty would be in laid up in a coma right about now. The whole crew was trying to finish the job for you. Cheno stopped them and saved the hoe."

Everything Breeze said after Quell was a blur. The nigga was fine, standing at least six feet two inches, two hundred forty pounds, chocolate, smooth skin, with a full beard. Whew, I knew staying away from him was imperative for me to do. The words he spoke outside the club echoed in my ears.

"Are you even listening to me?" Breeze smirked.

"Uh, what you say?"

"Nothing. The nigga upstairs in the other room if you were wondering. Go ahead and get that morning wood. I know you want it."

"I'm straight. I won't be the one to mess that man's life up like that. This pussy ain't for everybody. There's a lot of power in this muthafucka. I'm sitting on a goldmine and I won't be held responsible for the way he acts after the fact."

Breeze turned around and paused briefly then a devious grin spread across her face. "You mean to tell me you were locked up with actual clit baits and you didn't get down at least once."

"Hell nawl! Working on cars made my nipples hard. Those nasty bitches with their jailhouse dildos were putting their mouths on anything moving. Not my cup of tea. I was introduced to dick early on; cat was never on the menu for me. That's the reason I no longer desire Chinese food. I'm not eating no parts of a cat."

A pair of arms wrapped around my neck and something big, meaty, and thick rested against my back. The floodgates opened between my legs. Jaquellis smelled just as good as he did the night before even though he hadn't showered. His breath didn't stink either.

"I can introduce you to a lot more than dick," he whispered in my ear and his lips grazed my lobe making me squirm. "Do you have an extra toothbrush for me?"

I didn't know what was stocked in my own crib. The words were stuck in my throat and I couldn't even force out a response. His voice had me in a trance, clouding my brain. Cheno's voice brought me back to reality because I didn't know his ass stayed the night too.

"Nigga, get yo' ass off my people and where is yo' muthafuckin' shirt?" Cheno entered the kitchen pushing

Jaquellis away from me playfully. "You can find a toothbrush in the bathroom around the corner under the sink. How the fuck you in her face with dragon breath? Go clean yo'self up, Stinky."

Jaquellis chortled and winked at me while licking his lips. I watched him until he rounded the corner. The huge lion tattoo on his chest was beautiful. I envisioned running my tongue along the detailed image. Once again, Cheno's voice brought me back to reality.

"Stop depriving yo'self and live a little. I'm not saying marry the nigga, but have fun. He's really feeling you, Cuz."

"Nah, I'm good. Ya boy won't be popping up on me all the way from Dallas 'cause I'm not answering his damn calls. Honey don't play that. Where is Charlie?" I asked, trying to change the subject.

"Stay on topic, Honey. What if I told you Quell is moving here? Would you change your mind?" Cheno asked.

Breeze laughed hard as hell as she took two paninis from the sandwich maker then added two more. Then, she threw some fries in the oil on the stove. My stomach clinched tightly while trying my best not to show the concern I was having about the information Cheno laid on me. He waited patiently for me to respond and I obliged after a while.

"When did he decide to do that?"

"He wants to open another tattoo parlor here. Not too far from your business actually. Plus, I need him to help me sniff out the bullshit in my camp. Quell will be on the outside looking in before he joins my team, but I must get to the bottom of the problem at hand soon as possible."

"Wait, what problem are you referring to? Why didn't I know about it?" Breeze interjected.

"You left the shop before I could run it by you. I'll fill you in while we eat. Hurry the fuck up. A nigga hungry than a muthafucka."

Cheno sat down to bring Breeze up to speed on the happenings in the street. I sat daydreaming about Jaquellis. I was fighting his advances, but my kitty was ready to risk it all. Hearing he did tattoos excited me because I wanted some ink done.

I got up to leave the kitchen when Cheno yelled out to me. "Your stripper money is in the safe. I should've taken that shit. Dirty ass money."

"You knew better than to play with my bread. Cousin or not, I would've beat your body. Thanks though."

I left the kitchen and passed Taz coming down the stairs. I had to escape to my bedroom so I could compose myself. My second chance at life was looking up for the better.

Chapter 11

Cheno

Me and Quell left Honey's crib agreeing to meet up later. It took a lot for me convince Breeze not to go off the deep end about the robbery at my trap. She finally agreed to wait for me to reach out to her if needed. It was bad enough that I had her out in the street selling weed. The last thing I wanted was my sister pulling the trigga on these snake muthafuckas. My mother was probably rolling over in her grave for the choice I made to allow my sister to hustle. She didn't like the fact that I was doing it when she was on this earth. My phone rang with Charlie's name displayed on the dash. I knew she was about to be on bullshit because I didn't come home last night.

"What's up?" I asked pulling in our driveway.

"Where you at?"

"At the crib," I said shortly.

Charlie huffed loudly into the phone. "This the shit I be talking about! You lying like a muthafucka because I just checked the cameras and there's no movement in the house!"

"Check again, Inspector Gadget," I said walking over the threshold.

Charlie was irking the fuck out of me by trying to track my moves. She had every right. A nigga was out there bad to be honest. Don't get me wrong, I love Charlie, but I also have a connection with a couple of other females too. None of them would ever be my main woman. Charlie had that shit on lock. Bitches didn't know how to keep what we did behind closed doors to themselves. They always had to run their mouths as if they didn't know what it was from jump.

"I know you not just coming from Honey's house. Where you been, Cheno?"

"That's where I was, now I'm home. What do you want, Charlie? The bullshit you on is about to get yo' ass cussed out."

My patience was wearing thin at that moment because nobody was able to track down that nigga Tank. The whole setup had me looking at muthafuckas sideways. Honey's party took my mind off the shit that happened for the night. I couldn't let business mess up what I'd planned. Honey deserved to have fun after being cooped up under supervision for years. It was go time from now on.

"I don't want shit! If I find out you were with one of them bitches…"

"I'll talk to you later."

Ending the call in the most respectful way possible, I went into the bedroom taking my clothes off along the way. I got plenty of sleep on Honey's couch but my body felt like I hadn't slept in days. My mind was working nonstop trying to figure out how Tank was able to run up on my spot the way he did. The shit wasn't adding up.

I went into the bathroom and started the shower making the water hot as I could stand it then stepped in. I placed my hands on the wall while the steam surrounded me as my body slowly relaxed. Out of nowhere something clicked in my mind and I hurried to wash my ass. I jumped out, brushed my teeth, then threw a towel around my waist. As I passed the bed, I grabbed my phone and beelined to my office.

"The cameras, Cheno. I forgot about the muthafuckin' cameras!"

Tapping away on the computer, I had to retrieve my password because my stupid ass forgot what it was when I set up the system. My heart was beating a mile a minute as I waited for the site to load fully. When it was finally ready to go, I went to the drop tab and clicked on the day before and entered a time to start my search. Watching the footage, I sat down and waited for Lil Mike to appear. Everything he told me was the truth down to him talking to him talking to Ease. The cameras inside didn't tell me any more than I already knew. So, I went to the footage outside and went back a few days to see if I saw anything suspicious.

As I studied the footage day by day, there was nothing out of the norm taking place. Something told me to look into the evening hours because wasn't shit happening when the sun was shining bright. The first thing I noticed was an old school Chevy parked right outside the cameras frame on several occasions. The nigga Tank could be seen scoping my shit out for a whole week. Then somebody I couldn't identify walked out the trap and approached him. The two was very familiar with one another and it didn't seem as if there was any type of beef between them. That shit in itself rubbed me the wrong way. Just like I thought, somebody in my circle help that muthafucka hit my shit. Grabbing my phone, I called Ease.

"What up, Cheno?"

"Where you at, nigga? I need to holla at you."

"I'm about to head to the trap. Everything good? I heard about what happened yesterday."

"Yeah, that shit was fucked up. Don't go to the trap. Meet me at 7515 S. Drexel in an hour. I got a proposition for you."

"Oh shit! Say less. I'll be there. I need to call Free and tell him I'm meeting with you. I'm supposed to be filling in for Lil Mike since he's on suspension right now."

"You don't need to do that. I'm gon' make sure he knows. Beat me there, Ease."

"I got you, Bossman."

My blood was boiling from the footage I'd seen. When I eat, my entire team eats. Taking my workers off the payroll was a first for me and looking back at the footage reassured that I made the right choice. The niggas were slacking on all levels and I needed to call a meeting to lay down the ground rules once again because these muthafuckas thought chillin' with bitches, drinking, and not paying attention was part of their job description. All that shit was going to come to a halt when I finished with them.

Moving the crystal bowl I stored my weed in closer to me, I retrieved a wood from the drawer and rolled up a fat ass blunt. Inhaling the smoke, the shit burned because I held it in long as I could before letting it out through my nose. The betrayal hurt like hell and I could feel myself morphing into someone I didn't know. I've laid down plenty of niggas but I'd never had to kill one of my own. The ship I ran was tight; at least that's what I thought. But there was a first time for everything. I was ready to pay for the funeral for whichever nigga who thought he could bite the hand that fed his ass and thought he was still gonna be part of the family.

After finishing my blunt, I went to get dressed. Putting my Glock in the small of my back, I pulled my shirt down to conceal my weapon. I headed out the door and hopped in my Impala to meet Ease. The nigga had been on my team for a couple years and never moved recklessly. I put Ease on when he killed a muthafucka that was sneaking up on me after leaving Harold's on 87th. If it wasn't for him, I wouldn't be here today. I've never felt I owed another nigga shit, but I owed Ease and it was going to hurt my soul if I had to make him eat dirt.

The property on Drexel was a trap that I had an older lady named Pearl living to watch my shit. Pearl was an OG who would blast anybody that came through on any type of bullshit. She was actually the one who put me on. Pearl ran the southside back in the day and after her grandson Smurf was killed, she wanted someone just as big as him to run his territory. The day of my mother's funeral, Pearl paid her respects and showed me and Breeze so much love. Her and my mother went way back, but only communicated every so often because my mother didn't agree with the life Pearl lived. They stayed in touch and Pearl made sure my mama was straight even after we left the city. The proposition Pearl hit me with was one I couldn't refuse. It put me in a position to make more money than I'd seen while living down south.

"Boy, why you got people coming to my house?" Pearl called out from the front porch.

"Hey, granny," I said getting out of my whip.

"Don't hey granny me. Answer the damn question, Ricky."

Pearl using my government name let me know she was truly pissed. I saw Ease's truck parked in front of the house as I made my way to the stairs. Pearl was standing in wait and soon as I climbed the last step, she hit me upside my head.

"Ricky, you better tell me what I want to know. I don't know shit about the little fucker that's sitting in my living room. Who is he?"

"Calm down, Pearl. I had him to meet me over here because I couldn't talk to him at any of the known places. Your house was the best place to come to. A muthafucka named Tank hit my spot and I know it was an inside job. Ease was supposed to be at the trap that morning but he was told not to show up. I need to find out who made the call."

Pearl paced back and forth wearing the hell out of the slippers she had on her feet. She wasn't done fussing so I waited for her to finish thinking about what I'd just told her. It took damn near fifteen minutes and a Newport until she was ready. When she plucked the butt over the banister, I knew shit was about to get real.

"You mean to tell me there's a snake in your yard and you ain't did shit about it yet? When did this shit happen?"

"Yesterday morning," I replied.

"Why the fuck you didn't deal with it yesterday, stupid ass?"

"My cousin Honey came home yesterday and I had a lot of shit put together for her. Hell, she's been gone damn near a decade and I wasn't about to spoil her muthafuckin day. Any more questions, Pearl?"

"I know you not talking about Victoria's daughter, Honey."

"Yup. She's finally out of the system and I had to show her a good time. I made sure she was straight then we went out to celebrate her freedom. That was more important than chasing a ghost I didn't know shit about. Can I go in and handle this shit now?"

"Yeah, go on in. I want you to look out for that girl, Ricky. Her mama ain't shit for leaving her to do all that time by herself. Everybody knew James wasn't shit. I just didn't take him for the molester type. You the only family she has because Victoria don't claim Honey as her daughter. She needs you."

"What the fuck you mean you didn't take him for the molester type?" I sneered.

"Victoria told anybody who would listen that Honey accused her man of touching her. Then he was found murdered in an alley. She kicked her own daughter out of the house behind a nigga who was violating her. Victoria also said Honey was behind James' murder and that was why she was in prison. I know that was a lie because she was locked up behind Cheese punk ass. She must've forgot that anything that happens in the streets, I know about the shit."

"Well, where the fuck do a nigga named Tank live?"

"Tank? That's Verna's son. He will steal yo' draws if you don't get your legs in them fast enough. Did he have something to do with your trap getting robbed?"

"That nigga did it! Can't nobody find his ass though and Cheese talking about he don't fuck with his ass."

"You bet not believe that shit. Cheese knows where his cousin is and he's going to protect him off the strength of his aunt. I can't stand that bitch either. She lives out west on

Springfield. We'll talk about that later. Let's see what this muthafucka knows. If we have to kill his ass, so be it. I done told yo' ass to cut off the snake's head far too many times. I don't know what its gon' take to turn you into a monster, but I want you to practice right now."

Pearl led the way into her house and the aroma of good ole soul food smacked me in the face. In the kitchen, she could cook more than dope. Pearl was the grandma every nigga in the hood wish he had to put his feet under her table after running the streets all day. The smoked meat in the greens was potent as hell and I could taste the oxtails a mile away. Walking right past the living room, I was going in the direction my stomach guided me.

Ricky, business first!"

Pearl's voice stopped me in my tracks and I wanted to throw a tantrum like a toddler. Ease sat laughing as I entered the room he was in. He sat back on the couch when Pearl gave him an evil glare.

"Aye, Ease. Tell me what happened yesterday," I said standing over him.

"I called Mike to let him know I was on my way. I was running a little late, you know. He told me he would leave the door unlocked for me then hung up. I was around the corner from my crib when I got a text from an unknown number telling me not to go."

"Wait, you took the orders from a muthafucka you didn't know?"

"Nah, the end of the message had Fredo's name on it so, I figured it was him," Ease retorted.

"There's only three muthafuckas that can change the plans in our camp. You, Fredo, and Free. Cheno, I'm not stupid, man."

Ease didn't appear to be nervous, nor did he seem as if he was lying. I believed what he was telling me but it didn't get me any further to who was behind my shit getting hit. Fredo had been my righthand for years. Hell, he came to Chicago with me so there was no way he would stab me in the back by robbing my spot. The way niggas were moving nowadays, one could never know.

"Pull up the text," I snapped.

Without hesitation, Ease pulled his phone out and started scrolling then handed it to me. I read the text a few times. Sure enough, Fredo's name was at the bottom as a signature. The shit didn't sit right with me because the number wasn't one associated with him. I remembered the number then pressed the call icon. The phone rang but the voicemail picked up.

The caller you are trying to reach has a voicemail that hasn't been set up.

I gave the phone back to Ease and sat down. The mystery of the entire matter was consuming me and I didn't like that shit at all. I rubbed my hands together as I thought long and hard about how I needed to move. I cleared my throat, and turned my head toward Ease.

"I want you to report any and everything you see going on at the trap on the Nine. You on for seven until further notice. Do not say shit to nobody and if there's any questions about why you there, tell the muthafuckas to call me. This meetup didn't happen. Do you understand me?"

"I got you, Cheno. Fredo telling me not to come to the trap then it gets robbed. That nigga had something to do with that shit, huh?"

"Truth be told, I don't think Fredo had anything to do with what happened. That's what I need you to find out. Somebody in my circle is out to get me and when I find out, they are good as dead. You are not excluded."

"Me! I just told you what happened and I'm a suspect," Ease exclaimed.

"Until the snakes are lured out, everybody is questionable at this point," Pearl said putting her two cents in. "If you didn't have nothing to do with what went on, then you have nothing to worry about. Do what you were told and you live to see another day. Consider yourself a snitch from this point on because you better run your mouth like diarrhea when the time comes. I will personally come and blow your head off if I find out you were in on the bullshit. I may be old, but I'm the wrong bitch to fuck with."

"I believe you too, Miss Pearl. I promise, I didn't have a hand in this. Cheno made a way for me to eat and I've been standing solid ever since," Ease said. "Mike is innocent too. He looks up to you, Cheno."

"Only time will tell, Ease. You can head on to the trap. I'll be over there in a minute. Keep yo' eyes open, nigga." Ease got up and headed for the door after we dapped up. "I got some extra cash for you. Put yo' game face on. You gon' need it."

Ease opened the door. "Boy close that door! Get in here so I can fix you a plate of greens, pinto beans, oxtails with gravy and rice, candied yams, and cornbread. Cheno you ain't shit. The boy is shaking like a wet ass cat because he has to go against the street code, then you gon' send him out there on an empty stomach. That's grounds for him to get himself killed because he can't think straight."

I laughed because Pearl used every excuse in the book to feed some damn body. I didn't have to be invited to eat, I went into the kitchen and washed my hands before piling my plate with everything on the menu. She was right about not being able to think on an empty stomach. Soon as I put the first forkful in my mouth, my brain started working overtime.

Chapter 12

Tank

Yesterday I pulled the biggest job of my illegal career. Hitting Cheno's spot was the come up of the year. It was easy running up in the trap. The young nigga didn't put up a fight and that was the best move for him because I had plans to end his life. Cheno had a grimy muthafucka on his roster though. Without the help of his people, there would've been bloodshed for sure. That was one of the reasons I worked alone. You couldn't trust anybody in the streets.

I was sitting at the table running money through the counter and my dick got harder with every number change. Cheno took a major hit by my hands and I was proud. With the bricks alone, I was going to make about sixty thousand. The money was a bonus and so far, I was at thirty thousand dollars with one more bag to count. I dumped the ashes from the blunt I was smoking into an empty pop bottle then took a long pull. The alert of the alarm system sounded and I automatically grabbed my tool off the table and stood.

"Man, ain't nobody coming in here but me. This my crib, nigga! Put that shit down."

Seeing the nigga that put me on walk around the corner, I lowered my weapon. He was right that I was in his spot, but I wasn't going to take a chance with everything I'd done. The nigga opened one of his properties up for me to lay low until shit died down. I turned my phone off so I wouldn't be contacted by anybody until I decided to talk.

"Aye, Cheno got muthafuckas out looking for you. I thought you said nobody in the trap knew who you were."

"I don't know them niggas! Maybe they heard about me and what I do. I mean, I am the nigga that takes big shit that don't belong to me," I laughed.

"The shit ain't funny, Tank. You got a bounty on yo' head and you know how that shit can go. Cheno even found out your cousin is Cheese. This can cause a war between them two muthafuckas and they don't even have beef."

"What the fuck do that have to do with me? Ya boy better come correct when he go after my cuzzo. Cheese ain't a soft nigga. Fam will eliminate his whole crew and won't think nothing about it. Tell Cheno to choose his battles wisely because cuz don't play about me."

I flamed up another blunt while watching this nigga for any signs of deception. My gun was still close by, waiting for him to call himself cashing in on that bounty he talked about early on. I picked up a stack of bills and ran them through the counter.

"You didn't believe me when I said we had about a hunnid eighty grand altogether?"

"Nigga, I don't take the word of nobody but myself."

"Well, when you're finished playing banker, divide that shit up so I can get out of here. Another thing, don't bring nobody here because you are the only muthafucka that knows about this spot."

"I got you. If you scared of Cheno, say that," I cracked on his ass.

"Scared? That nigga don't put fear in my heart. Robbing his ass was minor. I got plans to end his muthafuckin' life."

Jealousy was the reason he was going after Cheno so hard. Greed got a nigga killed every time. It wasn't going to be long before Cheno found out which one of his soldiers were stabbing him in the back. The only way he didn't find out was if he wasn't as good as the people claimed he was. Me on the other hand, was going to see how far I could get by hitting his ass every chance I got. Cheno was going to be running like a track star trying to find me as I made his life a living hell.

"What did Cheno do to you? From the looks of it, the nigga out here getting money hand over fist."

"I want the top spot! The fuck you thought? I'm the muthafucka running his shit while he out here fucking anything with a pussy. Shid, I'm gon' go after his bitch too. Cheno don't know a good woman if it slapped him in the face. His girl is a diamond and she knows how to get a muthafuckin' bag. With a little tender lovin' care, she'll leave that nigga in a heartbeat."

There was no way Cheno didn't know how envious this dude was of him. The signs had to be visible at some point. Unless he was kissing the bottom of the boss' boot putting on a hell of a show, the venom was dripping of his lips with every word he spoke. I couldn't sit listening to his ass another minute. I rushed to count the rest of the money, then tallied up all the loot. In total we had two hundred and ten grand. The nigga was thirty thousand off and I was kicking my own ass for not counting the shit sooner. I could've got over on his stupid ass too. I counted out his half, put it in a duffle bag then bagged up my bricks along with forty-five thousand in cash.

"Aight, nigga. I'll be back to check on you soon as shit die down. Remember what I said about bringing muthafuckas here."

"I heard you the first time. See yo' way out because I'm tired as hell. Sleep is calling and I'm about to answer."

Waiting about a half hour after he left, I gathered my shit, and bounced out of his crib. I'd done what needed to be done. Protection from the opp was something a nigga like me didn't need. I jumped in my Chevy and headed to my hideaway in Bellwood. A muthafucka was far from broke.

Everybody who thought they knew me assumed I stayed with my mama. Including Cheese. One thing I always followed in life was when my mama told me to never let the left hand know what the right is doing. I was hardheaded than a muthafucka when it came to anything else she tried to instill in me. I hit the expressway smoking a blunt and blasting Jeezy's *Trap Star* all the way to the crib.

***

I woke up from a peaceful sleep I didn't know was needed. My mouth was drier than the Sahara Desert and I didn't want to get up to grab a bottled water from the kitchen. Cotton mouth is real and that shit had my tongue stuck in place without moisture. The therapeutic mattress I spent hundreds of dollars on had a strong hold on me as I struggled to get out of bed.

Cool air had me shivering as I made my way to the door. When I entered my house, it was hot as fuck due to me not being there for a while and the smoldering heat outside. I had no choice but to turn the air conditioning on if I didn't want to die from a heat stroke. After guzzling down the water, I grabbed another just in case and went back to my bedroom. I went into the bathroom to drain my pipe then washed my hands. Returning back to my bedroom, I got back in the bed. The lick I'd hit gave me the opportunity to take a couple days off.

I reached for my phone on the nightstand and powered it on. Notifications started going off back-to-back the moment the screen lit up. My mama was cussing me out as I listened to the many voicemails she had left for me. The phone was still going off as I opened my text messages. I should've been calling my mama back instead I went to the thread between me and Cheese. He had sent five messages and I wanted to see what he had to say. *Cheese: What the fuck you do?*

Cheese: Where you at?

Cheese: You got me caught up in yo' bullshit and Cheno on yo' head! Call me soon as you get this message.

Cheese: You better be dead! Ain't no way you just ignoring my calls and texts!

Cheese: If you don't hit me up by the end of the day, I'm painting this muthafuckin' city red!

Reading the messages had me holding my stomach laughing. Cheese was so damn dramatic at times and I blamed that shit on Letty's ass. She had Cheese softer than Cottonelle tissue. When he was with Honey, baby girl was thuggin' right by his side and beating ass along the way. Letty didn't know shit besides spending Cheese's money. Too bad Honey's fine ass was locked up. She would have Cheese back on his gangsta shit.

I decided to call Cheese to at least let him know I was still breathing. I flamed up because Cheese was going to blow the fuck out of me. My plan was to be high in the process so I wouldn't hurt his feelings for coming at me like he was my guardian. I may have been the younger cousin, but I was still a grown ass man holding shit down on my own. Smoking the blunt to the halfway point, I made the call to get that shit out of the way. Cheese answered with aggression.

"Nigga yo' mama worried about yo' stupid ass! She's been calling me crying thinkin' you dead or some shit."

"Man, stop hollerin' at me like I'm yo' child. You wanna use that tone, make a baby, nigga!" I snapped. "You muthafuckas know I'm straight, especially you. I do this shit on a regular and always come out on top. Cheno's trap ain't no different. Act like you know, Cuz."

"You fucked with the wrong one this time. That nigga not gon' take this loss sitting down. Word on the street, you hit him hard."

"Mission muthafuckin' accomplished. It look like Cheno got you niggas shook, walking around with y'all dicks tucked between ya booty cheeks. He bleeds the same way I do. The last thing I'm gon' do is fear a muthafucka. Yeah, he know I picked his pockets, do I give a fuck? Hell nawl! I'm ready for whateva. The nigga worried about the wrong shit. He need to be worried about the nigga that help me hit his spot."

Every breath Cheese took was heard loud and clear. He was pissed. I sat with my back against the headboard without a care in the world while getting lit. I was chiefing like a chimney. The smoke was thick and I loved every bit of that shit. Bishop from the movie *Juice* was how I was feeling after he killed Radames. The only difference, I'm a tough muthafucka with or without a gun and I ain't *never* let a soul punk me.

"You don't care about shit, do you? Cheno approached me at the club last night. I'm gon' ride with you, but we need to figure out how we gon' come at him."

"What you mean figure it out? If Cheno is the nigga he claims to be, he gon' strike first and then him and his crew gon' die by the hollows in my AK," I snapped back. "I think you need to let Letty go."

"How the fuck you go from yo' problem with Cheno to Letty?"

"I don't have a problem with that nigga. He got a problem with me. Anyway, I've told you time and time again you changed when y'all got together. Yo' ass ain't even hyped about handling Cheno's muthafuckin' ass. When you were with Honey, you went ape shit if somebody said yo' name wrong. Now, you wanna figure shit out rationally. Gon' get shot in the face trying to be Farrakhan, trying to talk this shit out. Get the titty out ya mouth so you can go back to being you."

"Fuck you! Letty ain't got shit to do with the way I conduct myself," Cheese sneered.

"Yeah, okay. Mad much?" I laughed. "When do Honey get out? She had ya back out here."

"Ain't nobody mad," he scoffed. "Speaking of Honey, she's out already. Her ass the reason her cousin walked up on me."

"Wait, my dawg out? Fuck that, who is her cousin?"

"Cheno! Didn't you hear me say that nigga approached me?"

"And I was supposed to know that was her people? Yeah, aight, I get it now. Honey the reason you trying to dance around this shit. Noted. I'm here to tell you when Cheno clap at me, believe it or not, you affiliated by association. Get ya mind right because you not safe either. The amount of money I racked up on this lick, I can bet on it that Honey ain't gon' be able to talk Cheno down to let this blow in the wind."

The weed had me laughing at the serious situation. It came off as a joke to me. It wasn't the case but Cheese didn't see it that way. I heard glass shatter on the other end of the phone, then his voice bellowed out in anger.

"This ain't funny! What the fuck you laughing for, stupid ass nigga? My better mind is telling me to leave you on yo' own."

"You can't!" I shouted. "The shit is very comical because you about to go after Honey and it ain't gon' work out in your favor. She ain't giving you another chance to disappoint her, Cheese. You left her behind the wall and started fucking her best friend! Make that shit make sense," I laughed harder. "The Honey I know gon' beat the fuck outta Letty every time she see her. And guess what? I blame you! Honey was solid as they come. She took a charge for you and the thanks she got was a few visits and a couple of bands on her commissary. That was a slap in the face. Leave that girl alone. She's gonna hate you more when I slump Cheno's bitch ass."

A call came in on my line as I ended the last statement. It was my mama's neighbor Miss Darlene.

"Hold on, Cuz." I swapped the call. "Hey, Miss Darlene. What's up?"

"Issac, get over here! Somebody done shot up Verna's house! The police and the paramedics are already in there with her."

Instead of going back to the call with Cheese, I ended the call and jumped up. Throwing on a pair of basketball shorts, a white tee, and a pair of Air Max. I snatched my keys and phone and made a beeline for the door. Locking up, I got into my whip and backed out of the driveway. My phone rang and it was Cheese.

"Get to my mama crib! Somebody wet her shit up. I'm on my way. Call me when you find out what's up if I'm not there in fifteen."

I broke every rule of the road and didn't give a fuck if the laws tried to pull me over. The muthafuckas was gon' have to chase me down all the way to my mama's crib because stopping wasn't an option. Weaving in and out of traffic, running red lights, and blaring my horn so stupid pedestrians could get the fuck outta my way, I hopped on the expressway. I got to my mama's house in record time and got out, running to the front door. The pigs were standing in front of my mama while Cheese cursed them out.

"Didn't she say she didn't know shit countless times?"

"I understand that. I need to make sure she's not in danger. A home riddled with so many bullets isn't coincidental. This was a targeted incident."

"Why would somebody want to shoot up the home of a woman in her fifties? What type of beef could she possibly have out here?" Cheese asked sarcastically.

"You have a point, but with relatives who are known as crooks, that could explain everything, LaDarrius," his partner smirked.

"Nigga, you don't know shit about me! Get the fuck out! The paramedics said she good so there's no reason for you to still be here."

I let Cheese deal with the pigs and I walked around them and sat next to my mama. She had a bandage on her arm and the shit pissed me off. I was grateful that she only had a minor injury, but she was touched and that shit had me thirty-eight hot. She looked at me then shook her head before turning her attention back to the police officers.

"Look, I don't know who shot up my house. My nephew and son don't even live here. They weren't present when all of this happened. While y'all in here interrogating me and my family, you should be calling whoever you need to and run those blue light cameras back. The citizens of Chicago are paying taxes out the ass for those things and nobody is ever arrested for the crimes committed. The shit isn't serving the purpose intended but they were installed to man the streets. Please leave my residence so I can get some rest."

"Miss Byrd, you were lucky to walk away with a graze wound. If you come across any additional information, please give me a call," the officer said holding out a business card.

My mama looked at him without taking it. He dropped the card on the coffee table, nodding. Cheese was already at the door holding it open for them to leave. Me on the other hand, I was preparing to roll up. Soon as the pigs was gone, my mama went in on my ass.

"Isaac, you know better than to have that shit in my house! I don't know what the fuck you have done, but you won't be bringing yo' bullshit here! I almost had a heart attack when all those bullets started coming through my windows. Leave my money on the table because I need to have all this shit fixed!" She yelled, poking me in the head with her finger.

"And La'Darrius, you selling all that dope on the street and this could have your name on it too. That poison is destroying people and all you're worried about is money! It's the root of all evil! I didn't just turn fifty years old to die. Y'all gotta stay away from here because I can't deal with this shit!"

I let my mama get everything she had to say off her chest. There was at least thirty holes in the walls throughout her crib. It didn't make sense for me to even fix the damage because she wasn't staying another day in that house. It was going to be hard for her to agree because she'd lived there for over twenty years, but I wasn't giving her a choice.

"Look, I don't know who came through here on bullshit. Excuse my language. You can't stay here because obviously it's not safe," I said licking the wood closed.

"This my house! I'm not letting these lil motherfuckers run me out of a place I put my blood sweat and tears in. You think I haven't heard about you stealing from folks, I see. I've known about that shit for years and it's the main reason I make sure the insurance is paid for both of you idiots! As a matter of fact, you stole from a deadly man just the other day and he and his hoodlum friends is probably who shot up my house! I'm not leaving, but you are!"

"Auntie——"

"Shut up, La'Darrius because if my sister was still walking this earth, your ass would be kicked ten times over! We didn't raise y'all to be running around slanging dope and being a stick-up king! That shit is dangerous and now my house has been targeted all thanks to y'all!"

"You gotta leave. We don't know if they will come back and finish the job or not. Just come stay with me until I can find you another house to live in," Cheese pled.

"Come live with you? That won't happen because you and all of the westside know I don't like that money hungry bitch you call your woman. In my opinion, you should've waited for Honey because she ain't it. But forget I said anything because I promised to never say anything about the hoe. Okay, that was the last time."

I looked at Cheese saying I told you in my head. My mama spit the real to his ass and I bet he still wasn't comprehending. That was his problem though. I had to get my mama to agree to jump ship. I was surprised she knew about my dealings in the street, then again, I wasn't because Miss Darlene's grandkids gave her the scoop on everything they heard about.

"Ma, that ain't even what we talking about right now. Let me put you up in a hotel until I can get the damage repaired."

"Can you hear, boy? I'm not going nowhere! Call somebody to fix my windows for the time being. It's early enough to get that done. Then go to Lowes or Home Depot and get me another door and two screen doors with deadbolt locks for the front and back doors."

"I can get that done today, but I'm staying here with you. It's not safe for you to stay in this house by yo'self."

"Once y'all finish with what needs to be done, there's no need for either of you to be here. Don't say shit else about it because y'all making my ass itch."

She got up, stormed out of the living room, and slammed the door to her bedroom. Cheese stood leaned against the wall tapping away on his phone. I stood taking the blunt from behind my ear and made my way to the backyard to smoke."

"I called Mack to watch the crib until we get back," Cheese said walking in my direction.

"Auntie Verna trippin'."

"Nigga, you just mad because she called Letty out. They say a mother can see shit we don't. You better listen."

"She ain't my mama though."

"May as well be. She will still whoop yo' ass," I laughed. "My mama punked that ass. The look on yo' face was priceless."

"Fuck you! Light that shit up. I need to take a deep pull off that muthafucka."

I laughed to keep from crying because the thought of them niggas killing my mama hurt my heart. There was no doubt about who was behind the madness. I had to take Cheno seriously and stop underestimating his reach and learn everything I needed to know about him and his operation.

Chapter 13

Honey

"Thanks for believing in me, Honey. When I customized my whip, it was just something I wanted to do for myself. Now, I get to put in major work and make a name for myself."

"I have faith in you and will back you one hundred percent. Generational curses stop with us. You and Cheno are the only family I have. We're in this thang together."

Breeze and I were standing in the middle of the room I'd designed for her to customize vehicles. The building Cheno had built for me was huge and he left two rooms unoccupied for whatever I decided to turn them into. For thirty days I taught myself how to wrap vehicles and I practiced on Breeze's Camero until I perfected it. The matte ultramarine color she chose was lit. The sun made the color pop then at night it looked midnight black. When I first sat in her car, I noticed the add-ons she had done then asked her who did the install. Upon learning she did them herself, I made a proposition she couldn't refuse.

I ordered all the equipment and just like that, wrapping and custom compartments were part of the business. Creating a social media page for Honey's Customization, I spread the word about all the services that were available. The picture of Breeze's whip from the wrapping to the hidden compartments were the main attractions. Niggas were all over it. I had a fifty percent sale for two weeks and the rest was history. The waiting list was long as hell even at full price everybody and their mama was trying to get this work. My paper chase was in full effect. Making a name for myself and the other women I had under my belt was a must and we were on our way.

"You do know we have more family here, right?"

"No disrespect, Breeze. I don't know them people. Nobody from my daddy's side other than your mother ever told me happy birthday, Merry Christmas, or shit. That's you and Cheno's family. They don't exist in my world. I'm sure all of them knew about my incarceration. Who reached out?"

"I get it. You have every right to feel the way you do. Give it some thought, we have cool ass cousins and you should meet them," Breeze said going across the room to admire the equipment.

Taz entered with a bouquet of roses, three Giordano's pizzas, and a large tin of Garretts popcorn in her hands. I smiled at Breeze because it was cute how she and Taz showered each other spontaneously. Placing the items on the work table, Taz handed the roses to me.

"Huh? This has to be a mistake," I said surprised.

"Nah, your name is on the receipt for the pizza and the envelop attached to the roses," Taz grinned. "Somebody has a secret admirer."

The relationship between me and Taz acquired in the last month or so has been so much better. Whatever Breeze said to her the day they stayed at my house must've made Taz think about her actions towards me. I liked the woman she was when she wasn't upset. She was very ugly otherwise.

I admired the flowers and loved the arrangement. The mixture of red and white roses with several baby breaths in between were beautiful. Whomever sent the delivery knew what I liked. One of the pizzas was thick crusted with spinach, mushrooms, onion, green peppers, and cheese. I stopped eating pork the moment the judicial system forced me into confinement. The other two were sausage and pepperoni. Racking my brain as I tried to figure out who could have done this for me, no one came to mind. Confusion had to be written on my face because Breeze spoke up.

"Read the card, Cuz. It will tell you exactly who's steppin' to you like a man or woman supposed to," she smirked.

"Stop playing with me, Breeze. Ain't no damn woman coming for me like that."

Both she and Taz had a field day laughing at me as I slowly opened the envelope. Taking a deep breath, my hands shook a little because I was nervous. I eased the card out as I blinked several times before finally reading the message.

Hey, Beautiful,

I love that smile lol. This is my way of telling you that I've thought of nothing except Honey Love since I left Chicago. I respect that you don't want to be attached to anyone, but you didn't say anything about a nigga courting you until the time is right for you. There's more where this comes from. Fix yo' face, Honey. Let me do what I do because you will be my lady. See you soon.

Quell.

"Okay, who is Mr. Mysterious? That smile is screaming a thousand words but you haven't opened your mouth."

I could feel my cheeks heating up and I knew I was blushing something terrible. Quell was still shooting his shot even though we hadn't spoken since he left my home months prior. I've thought about him as well a time or two, but refused to ask Cheno to contact Quell for me. My cousin was playing ghetto cupid. What other way would Quell know what to buy for me? His ass was from Texas.

"It's Jaquellis," I admitted to Breeze.

"Let me see what he said." Breeze said taking the card from my hand. She was so damn nosy.

"Girl, you better hop on that before one of these thirsty bitches dig their claws in him. Quell wants you, Honey. Give him a chance."

"No! I'm not playing into this with you and Cheno. Jaquellis is cool. We can only be friends. That's it, that's all. The gesture was very thoughtful and it did make me smile, I'm not ready to date."

"Honey——"

"Nope. Nope. Nope. Help me eat this pizza and popcorn so we can get back to work. Taz, tell everybody to come eat. You have someone coming in soon, right?" I asked Breeze.

"My nigga Coo coming through at one. I have a half hour," she said glancing at her watch.

We all sat around eating and enjoying being off our feet for a little while anyway. A family is the bond we had created since working hard together. Everyone got along without all the bickering, bitching, and attitude which usually stood between a group of women. None of that existed within the walls of the shop. At least at the moment. The bell chimed causing Tiny to head up front.

"Congratulations on bringing your vision to life. There are so many people who do time and act like their lives are over. Not you. The way you have been grinding toward the bag is admirable. All the niggas about to be running through here."

"Spank, you ain't happy for Honey. You ready to meet a new muthafucka to play with," Charlie joked.

"Hell yeah! I'm with you when you're right. I am happy about her newfound success and meant every word I said. We're about to shut every damn business down by stealing their customers. We provide everything from Oil changes to vehicle wraps right here. This a one stop shop baby and it's ran by a bunch of females!"

We all screamed, "You knowwwww!" as tiny's voice came through the intercom loud and clear.

"Breeze, you better come get this bitch before I hurt her!"

I was the first to leave the room wiping my hands on a napkin with what sounded like a herd of elephants behind me. The commotion grew louder the closer we got to the entrance. The female I saw eyeballing Breeze at club Déjà vu was cursing Tiny out rudely. Another woman was standing guard behind her friend and I knew shit was going to go left.

"Go get my bitch now!"

"Sia, I ain't never been yo' bitch. You were mine," Breeze seethed with Taz by her side. "What the fuck is yo' problem?"

"I knew you were fuckin' this hoe! Every time I asked about her you always made it seem like I was the insecure one. Friends my ass! I saw ya'll all hugged up, skinning and grinning in each other's face at the club. You lucky I didn't fuck this bitch up that night!"

"Slow that shit down, Shawty. Me and you ain't together no more. Why the fuck you trippin'? It doesn't matter who I'm with, it's not you," Breeze said calmly. "Bringing this bullshit to my cousin's establishment wasn't very bright."

"Why her? You know I love you. We should be together," Sia cried.

"Why not," Breeze chuckled. "You know exactly why me and you are no longer an item. Raise the fuck up out of here before I embarrass yo' ass."

"Please, Bre. I'm sorry." Breeze shook her head no while Sia sobbed. "I loved you more than I loved myself. We had so many plans in place and you just moved on to the next bitch. Here's your money so we can go back to being happy."

Sia realized Breeze wasn't feeding into her emotional break down and took it a step further. She got down on her knees in front of Breeze and held on to her pants leg. Trying to free herself, Breeze stepped back but Sia wasn't giving up.

"Ain't shit happening. I don't give second chances and I told you what to do with the money months ago. I'm done and there's no coming back."

"Please, Breeze."

"Sia, get up! You don't have to beg no damn body to be with you," Sia's friend yelled at her.

Charlie reached down to help Sia to her feet. I didn't say shit because it wasn't my fight. Breeze wasn't elevating the situation; she was trying to avoid it altogether. The way Breeze looked down at Sia held no remorse. She was fighting hard not to say anything to the friend and it showed the way her jaw clenched tightly.

"Bitch, don't touch her!"

"She's trying to help your friend save face and to escort her out of my shit," I interjected. "You said that shit with your chest like you know my sis or something."

"No, I don't know her. I know her man," she simpered. "Instead of worrying about Sia, she needs to pay attention to Cheno being gone and in my bed two to three nights out of the week. On top of that, I know Miss Charlie is tired of being the laughing stock in the streets."

I tried to block Charlie's path but she dodged me and Breeze. She was on baby girl like flies on shit, wearing that ass out. Blood flew from the girl's mouth as she swung wildly to protect herself. The way Charlie threw those haymakers took me back to our prison days. I grabbed my friend around her waist to separate them but I failed miserably. Charlie was locked in. The rest of the crew helped me get them apart then out f nowhere, Sia hit Charlie on the side of her head. Breeze yoked her up by the throat and walked out of the front door. I was winded from trying to hold Charlie, but ol' girl wouldn't shut the fuck up.

"Bitch, I bet not see you again because it's on sight. You put yo' hands on the right one today!"

"Whenever you ready," Charlie beamed. There's plenty more knuckle sandwiches where those came from. I'm down for whatever. You may want to get that knot checked between your eyes though."

Spanky pushed the girl until she was at the door. That didn't stop her from pouring more salt into Charlies wounds. The gleam in her eye told me some foul shit was about to come out of her mouth.

"You'll see me again, Charlie. Tell our man Larisa said hello and his pretty lips looks forward to cummin' in his mouth. Keep him warm for me," she winked then blew a kiss over her shoulder.

"Get the fuck out of here!" Spanky pushed Larisa out the door causing her to fall on her ass.

"It's bitches like you that end up on a flyer. Come back and you will deal with me. Stupid ass. I've never seen a female so proud to come second to a nigga who uses her for a cum bin."

Larisa was screaming obscenities as I pulled Spanky out of the doorway. Drama was the last thing I needed while trying to push my business to another level. The shit that Charlie was dealing with was another reason I didn't want to give my all in a relationship. Larisa and Cheno would be dead and I would be right back in jail if I was in Charlie's shoes. Looking around for my girl, she was nowhere to be found. The door opened and I damn near broke my neck hoping like hell Sia and Larisa was coming back for round two. Instead, a guy walked in smoothly.

"May I help you," I greeted him with a smile.

"That's my homie Coo. I got him, Honey," Breeze stepped in. She guided me away from Coo to talk privately. "Find Charlie and make sure she's okay. If what that hoe Larisa said is true, Cheno fucked up for the last time. There's just so much one can take when the other party continuously steps out on the relationship. He's about to lose her."

Nodding in understanding I let what Breeze said marinate. My mind went back to the day I was released and Charlie snapped on Cheno about a female that approached her. I never asked Charlie what was going on because it wasn't my business. Now, she had to explain everything to me from the top so I could try my best to prevent something bad from happening to either of them.

"Have him to pull his car around back and do yo' thang. I'll deal with Charlie. Do not call Cheno about this shit. Let me handle it."

Breeze walked off without a rebuttal and I hoped she would listen. Customers started coming in putting everybody back into work mode. I was very happy for the distraction. After making sure everything was being handled accordingly, I vowed to return once I checked on Charlie. When she was pissed off it was hard to bring Charlie down. Things were about to go from sugar to shit when it came to Charlie and Cheno. Or maybe it was already a disaster ready to happen and I'm just late to the show.

Chapter 14

Charlie

Cheno and his promiscuous ways had my blood boiling over like rice in a pot. I was tired of random bitches being able to walk up on me then gloat in my face. Everybody knew Charlie but my stupid ass was Ray Charles to the bullshit until somebody wanted to reveal the extracurricular activities they were indulging in with my man. For years I'd been beating hoes upside the muthafuckin' head behind Cheno. There was nothing he could say to make me stay this time around. It was time to move on from this toxic shit we called love.

I locked myself in the office bathroom to hide from the embarrassment I'd endured in front of everybody. I cried so much my eyes were puffy and my nose was redder than Rudolph's. Splashing water on my face, I anticipated Breeze knocking on the door to cuss me out. She loved her brother. In fact, she was Cheno's keeper, but one thing Breeze had never done was covered up his bullshit. She actually told me on several occasions to leave Cheno a long time ago. That thing called love forced me to stay. At this point, what's love got to do with it when I was the only participant that was putting in my all.

Remaining faithful wasn't an option, it was a priority in my world. Loyalty and respect were everything in a relationship. Cheno didn't appreciate all the love I'd shown him privately and in public so, it was time for me to jump ship. He got comfortable playing in my face because I allowed him to do it. Not anymore. He wanted to be in the streets, then the streets and the hoes could have him.

Knock. Knock

"Charlie, are you in there?"

Honey asked while jiggling the knob. Hearing her voice caused my eyes to well up with tears once again. I was happy she came for me instead of Breeze. There was a chance for me to explain how I was feeling to a neutral person. Honey didn't know anything about what had been going on between Cheno and I. Far as she knew, we were happy and in love. Which was farfetched and not true at all. I still had much love for Cheno, but we hadn't been happy in a long time and it was due to him fucking anything that moved with a pussy. But he loved me.

"Charlie, open the door! I can hear you sniffling."

Ignoring her was inevitable. I took tissue from the roll and blew my nose. As I passed the mirror I glanced at my reflection and cringed. Sadness didn't look good on me. My heart was broken and bruised, but at the same time I was angry. After taking a few breaths, I unlocked the door and left the bathroom. Walking pass Honey, I sat in the chair across from the desk.

"Talk to me. What's going on with you and Cheno?"

"I'm tired of him, Honey. I'm done."

"How you know she not lying? Bitches jealous out here every day, Charlie. Talk to him."

"She ain't lying about shit!" I jumped to my feet. "The muthafucka calls my pussy pretty lips all the got damn time! I thought the shit was cute, but I guess all coochie is pretty to his ass. This ain't the first time a female has thrown what they got going on with your cousin! But it's gon' be the last."

I got up and grabbed my purse from the desk drawer, gave Honey a hug and walked out with her following right behind me. Leaving work early was something I had never done since running the shop, but going home to pack my shit was my first priority. Cheno wouldn't be home so it was a good time for me to do what needed to be done peacefully.

"Charlie, where are you going?" Honey asked.

"To move my shit out of this nigga crib. You thought I was playing?" Charlie laughed.

"Wait a minute," she said grabbing my forearm. "Where are you going to live?"

"I'll figure it out after I pack. Maybe I'll get a hotel room until I'm able to find an apartment. I'll be straight. The bitches outside of my household need Ricky, I don't. I've been going through this shit too long not to be prepared to move around on my own. He lost a real on and Cheno will need an oxygen tank once he finds out."

"I'm about to call him."

"You will do no such thing! Fuck Cheno!" I yelled in Honey's face. "Did he call and tell you when he was penetrating these nasty bitches? Did he give me a heads up every time he had me out here looking like a clown? No, he didn't! If yo' cousin show up at the house, you better get ready to bury his ass because he will meet his maker. And I stand ten toes down on that!"

Yanking away from Honey I stormed out of the shop. One would think she'd leave me alone, but that wasn't the case. When I got inside my car Honey stood at the window. I started the engine and lowered the window without looking in her direction.

"Charlie, you can stay with me. I have more than enough room."

"Cheno has access to your home and I don't want to bring the drama to your doorstep. I'll be good. I promise to call when I'm settled." A lone tear slid down my face and I quickly wiped it away. "Honey, this has nothing to do with you and I'm sorry if I sound upset with you. All my anger is aimed at Cheno and Cheno only. Once I calm down, I'll go into more detail about what I've been through. Right now, I need to go."

"Okay. Don't forget to call me."

Shifting the gear into reverse I backed out of the parking lot. Past incidents played in my mind while I drove through the streets. When I hit the expressway my foot pressed on the gas, I clenched the steering wheel tightly, and made my way to the south suburbs to close the chapter of my life that I thought would be forever.

***

I'd been in the house over an hour and damn near had everything I owned in the back of my SUV. I planned to leave my car in the driveway and trade it out for my truck. The Airbnb I was able to make a down payment on for thirty days was booked. Taking all of my belongings to a hotel wasn't ideal to me so I had to make sure I would be comfortable. As I was packing the last of my toiletries, I heard the front door slam and heavy footsteps running up the stairs.

"Charlie! Charlie, where you at?" Cheno's voice roared.

Ignoring him I continued packing. He appeared in the doorway of the bedroom with a scowl on his face. Cheno looked around the room then walked into the closet. When he emerged, his head dropped to his chest. I could see his movements through the mirror.

"Come on man, we ain't doing this."

"You may not be, but I am. You wanna fuck around, now you can do it in peace. Nothing you say will change that."

"Larisa is somebody that sucked my dick…"

"The same dick you put in me raw! The same dick I choke on when it's deep down my throat! I need to go get tested because that bitch look like she wear cum as foundation on her muthafuckin' face! Ain't no telling how many niggas she fuckin' while waiting to *suck yo' dick!* You may not give a fuck about your health, but I value mine. I've told yo' hoe ass time and time again if you didn't want to be tied down, leave me the fuck alone! But each time you were sorry. Well, guess what? You are indeed a sorry muthafucka who has lost the realest bitch on your roster."

"I don't give a fuck about these other females. Who do I come home to every night, Charlie?"

"Are you for real?" I laughed. "Just because you bring yo' ass home justifies what you do on the other side of that door? You shouldn't be doing shit with nobody outside of me! I'm out here wearing yoke on my face because I'm screaming *my man, my man, my mannnnnnn* loud as hell but my nigga ain't solely my nigga!"

Cheno wrapped his arms around my waist burying his face into the side of my neck. I pushed back and slapped the taste out of his mouth drawing blood. He touched his lip and blood coated his fingertips.

"We don't do that hitting shit. Keep yo' hands to yourself, Charlie. Whatever Larisa said to you is a lie."

"How the fuck she lying when you said she sucked your dick? If you let it get to that point, you fucked. The bitch even told me the truth by saying your pretty lips will be waiting for you. Nigga, you say that shit to my pussy when you tongue deep in my shit! That damn girl ain't lying! But you got it, playboy. Do yo' thang because I'm out."

I grabbed my makeup case and the toiletry bag from the dresser. Cheno snatched the items from my hand and threw them on the bed. Easing my keys into my pocket, I nodded as he turned to face me while backing up toward the door.

"We said we were forever. You can't leave me like this." Cheno looked pitiful but that shit wasn't moving me. He clasped my hand tightly and I tried to yank it back; Cheno didn't let go. "I love you, Charlie. I'm sorry. This shit won't happen again."

"I've heard that same song and dance one too many times. It's not going to work this time. Three strikes and you're out is what they say. Nigga, I've given you too many first downs. It's my time to score the touchdown. This isn't where you want to be so I'm willing to let you live your life anyway you see fit. It just won't be with me."

Cheno kissed the back of my hand with tears in his eyes. Rubbing his thumb across the spot, he took a few deep breaths. "I will kill any nigga I see in yo' muthafuckin face, Charlie. Don't test me. I love you. This is not the end and we are just separated. I'm coming back for what belongs to me. Don't get too comfortable. Get yo' mind right because this shit is temporary. "

The words Cheno spoke came a little too late because I wasn't trying to hear anything coming from his mouth. Entertaining another man after leaving Cheno wasn't even on my mind. I wanted to focus on myself because Cheno and his lack of devotion took over my life. He saved me from the abandonment of my parents and I was forever grateful, but that didn't mean I was obligated to continue sitting back while he disrespected me without remorse. Cheno appeared to be sorry knowing I was leaving. It didn't seem sincere at all. What I got from his little speech was, I'm gonna say whatever will make her stay.

I retrieved my belongings and walked out without another word. As I walked down the stairs, I heard Cheno yell, *fuck* followed by the shattering of glass. He did this. Cheno couldn't blame anyone but himself. I didn't care if he burned the house to the ground. At this point, he could've been inside when it was all said and done.

I closed the back door of my truck and climbed into the front seat. Soon as I started the engine, Cheno rushed out pulling on the handle. I stepped on the gas and eased out of the garage. He started beating on the window aggressively and I peeled off with the quickness. I glanced in the rearview mirror and Cheno stood watching the back of my truck disappear down the street.

I arrived at the Airbnb and started unpacking my truck. My phone was ringing off the hook and I ignored it because I knew it was Cheno. I didn't have time to listen to him moan and groan about missing me, the house wasn't the same without me, I'm his rib. Blah, blah, blah. It took for me to leave for him to realize what I meant to him. Oh well.

"Allow me to help you with that," a voice behind me said. I turned to see who it was and my mouth dried instantly. Another man had never caught my attention since Cheno was all I saw. This man was fine and it should've been against the law for him to be out and about without a shirt. The muscles of his pecs bulged outward nicely. His abs were tight as leather and was sculpted like a masterpiece of art. I was lost in his physique and it made me feel as if I was cheating even though I'd just walked away from the relationship I was in. Dark skinned men never appealed to me, but this man was built like a God.

The sun glistened off his sweaty skin causing my eyes to follow a stream of sweat. It disappeared into his basketball shorts and the bulge was amazing. The wood was solid and curved to the left leaving nothing to my wild imagination. Shaking my head no, I finally found my voice after swallowing multiple times.

"I can handle it. Thanks, though."

"Well, welcome to the neighborhood. My parents taught me how to be a gentleman early on.

So, I couldn't just watch you lift all those boxes without offering help. I'm Ceasar by the way."

"Nice to meet you."

I didn't plan to see him again so I didn't offer my name. Instead, I took the box inside and dropped it by the door. When I returned to my truck, Ceasar was leaning against it. Chuckling to myself, I licked my lips slowly moving forward.

"Is there something I can help you with?" I asked reaching inside to grab another box.

"Yeah, I was wondering, will you be interested in going to dinner with me tonight? I mean if you're up to it after settling in of course."

"I'm sorry, but no. Not to be rude or anything but I just ended a long relationship. Starting something new wouldn't be wise right now."

"I truly understand. Whoever this dude is, fucked up a good thing. There's no way I would've ever let you go."

"How do you know I wasn't the cause of the breakup? You immediately blamed the man."

Ceasar stood tall rubbing his hands together. He stared intensely at me as if he was trying to read into my soul. I was very intrigued to hear what his response would be.

"I am ninety percent sure he was the reason. I was admiring you from afar for about six minutes before I approached you. No, I wasn't stalking the new woman on the block. My second lap into my run actually was interrupted by your beauty. Anyway, I heard your phone repeatedly ring while Inayah's "For the Streets" blared from it. I'm very familiar with that song and the lyrics told me all I needed to know. The only thing missing is you having a new man. I can help you with that."

I laughed because his observation was on point. Ceasar was putting it on thick. Not enough to persuade me to go out with him though. He was easy on the eyes, in shape, and very funny. The words Cheno said played in my head. *I will kill every nigga I see you with.* I believed he would do that shit and get away with it, too. There was no way I could put Ceasar in that position.

"You don't want to deal with me. My ex is crazy and I won't subject you to my past."

"I won't push you any further, Beautiful. I'm a short walk away if you need anything."

"I'm sure I won't, but thanks," I said heading back to the house.

Hurrying to get back outside to see how close Ceasar actually lived to me, I was taken back when I noticed him going right into the house next door. Avoiding him was going to be hard because he could see as I came and went at all times. Ceasar was going to be a problem once my kitty started purring. Going back to Cheno wasn't in my plans. Hopping on a new pogo stick was probably something I could test out in the future. Being forty-five minutes away from the home I shared with Cheno, bumping into him was unlikely but not impossible.

I unloaded the last of the boxes and finally locked up the house then set the alarm. Downers Grove was nothing like the city but one could never be so sure the way crime had hiked around the world. Folks were going insane by the minute and I'd rather be safe than sorry. Looking around at all the boxes, it was about to be a long rest of the day and I couldn't wait to eat and crawl in the bed.

Chapter 15

Cheno

Breeze called cursing me out about Larisa showing her ass at Honey's shop. I wanted to tell my sister to stay the fuck out of my business but I knew how she felt about Charlie. Nobody could tell Breeze that she was not her real sister. She loved Charlie just as much as I did and their relationship never wavered. Hell, Breeze was in the street helping Charlie beat bitches then chewed my ass out after the fact. It was no different this time.

I stood on the block listening to everything that went down without interrupting Breeze once. I deserved all the fuck nigga references, telling me my dick was going to fall off, and the bitches I was cheating with being described as gold diggers. All that shit went in one ear and out the other until Breeze told me Charlie left the shop to pack and leave our home. I hopped in my whip and tore ass to my house.

When I pulled into the driveway. I spotted her car and sighed with relief that it was empty. As I thought, Charlie wasn't going any fuckin' where. I sat for a few minutes thinking about how I was going to convince her to stay this time. Once I entered the home, I noticed the door leading to the garage was opened. It piqued my curiosity causing me to see what was going on out there.

Charlie's truck was filled to capacity with bags and boxes and my heart sank to my ass. I slammed the door and ran upstairs. I tried throwing everything at Charlie except the kitchen sink and she dodged all that shit. I even came clean about Laris sucking my dick but Charlie is far from stupid. Me and Laris fucked indeed. In fact, I was at her apartment breaking her back in every chance I got. Revealing that shit would've been an instant trip to the hospital. I was lucky all Charlie did was bust my lip. She almost got her ass beat. I just couldn't bring myself to put my hands on her for finding out I stepped out on her... again.

It was only right for me to allow her to walk out on our relationship to get her mind right. Charlie had me fucked up if she thought this shit was over for good. She was lucky I needed to deal with the bullshit with Tank or I would've fought harder. With Charlie out of the way, there was a huge chance she wouldn't get caught up in the bullshit behind me shooting Tank's mama's house up. My actions forced me to close down the trap on the Nine but that didn't put a dent in my pockets. Business was still booming better than ever.

Cheese sent a message by shooting at my young soldiers two days later. He lost a couple of his people but mine was alive to live another day with minor wounds. The day of the funerals will be remembered by all in attendance because I disrupted the mourning process with a stream of bullets. I didn't have any intentions to kill anybody, but I riddle those caskets up so they would have to dish out more money. Also, I wanted them niggas to know all eyes were on their ass and they're lucky I had a heart and Tank's mama was still breathing. I learned the other day she was still living in the same spot. Tank must think I won't hit the bitch house again. He had another thing coming because if he didn't bring me my shit, I will finish what I started.

It's been two weeks since Charlie left a nigga and she still wasn't answering my calls. No matter how many times I reached out to her, she didn't block me. I took that as a sign that she still loved me. I sat on the side of my bed tying up my black Jordan Retros. Pairing them with a black tank, and black jean shorts, I added my black fitted hat to set the outfit off. It was eight-five degrees and the day for our fifth annual adult biker block party.

The party was a way for any and everybody to showcase their motorcycles while having fun doing it. I was able to shut South Chicago down from 77th to 79th so we could celebrate without the traffic. Many of the citizens complained about the road blockage but my money talked louder than their complaining asses. My phone sounded and I snatched it up from the bed.

"What's up, Sketty?"

"Everything is set up. Shree brought the food, Fredo and Hank got us right with the alcohol. Free ain't here yet."

"Aight, I'm heading out now. Y'all keep trying to get in touch with Free."

"I got you, Cheno. We about to turn the fuck up! See you when you get here."

"Aye! Is the DJ there?"

"Of course. Juke been spinnin' for a half hour. He got the folks occupied until you get here. You know how he do."

"My nigga. I'll be there soon." Ending the call I grabbed my phone, keys, and wallet before leaving my bedroom. I entered the garage and smiles at the tarp on the other side of the space. I had waited all year for the moment to take my baby out to play. Unveiling my Suzuki GS1300R I stepped back and whistled. Honey hooked my bike up with a black and white wrap on top of customizing my name with fire on the side. The shit was cold.

When Honey told me what she wanted to do, I was against it until she challenged me to designed my bike. It took a few days to agree because my motorcycle was my pride and joy. The end result was one I was wrong to doubt. My cousin was going far with the addition to her business. If she thought the shop was busy now, it was going to be a thousand times busier after niggas see the work she put in on my shit.

I couldn't wait to see Charlie. With Honey never attending one of my events, there was no way Charlie wouldn't show up with her. Bowing my head before I mounted my bike, I took a minute to talk to the OG above. Being a nigga who did wrong on a daily, I still had God to have my back. I prayed for him to cover me and everybody who would be in attendance for the day. I wasn't naïve there was a huge chance some shit could pop off and I wanted to be prepared. Everybody and their mama showed up every year and this one wouldn't be any different.

After I said Amen, I got on my bike, put my Air pods in my ears, and kicked the stand off the ground. The engine roared as the garage door rose. Soon as I was able, I revved out onto the driveway pushing the button on my keys to secure my home. Kevin Gates' *Thinking with My Dick* came on. I laughed because it was ironic to hear that particular song because that was the reason Charlie wasn't fuckin' with me. My dick led me in several directions when I should've left that muthafucka locked away at the crib.

Weaving through traffic I arrived on South Chicago in record time. I pulled a few feet away from the DJ table on the 79th Street end of the party. Females called out when they saw me. For the first time that thirsty shit irritated my soul. It was too late to control how I interacted with these bitches, but I had to do whatever it took to prove I only wanted Charlie.

"What up, nigga?" Fredo asked dapping me up then turning to my bike. "That muthafucka go hard! Honey did that?"

"Yeah, Cuz doing her shit," I boasted. "It's thick than a bitch out here."

"You know how we do. Best event of the year, nigga. It's gon be memorable fo' sho'." Fredo stated. "Aye what's up with Free? He didn't answer when I called. Something ain't right with him. No bullshit, brah. He been movin' funny since the trap got hit." He flamed up and took a long toke of a blunt.

"When you came to me about hittin' Bam up that day, I was confused because that shit never took place. A muthafucka playing on my top and I think it's Free. Cheno, we've been down with each other since we were shorties. Nowadays that don't mean a damn thang but nothing would ever make me snake a muthafucka who put me in the position I'm in. You treat me better than my blood family and I'm riding with you 'til the end. The truth gon' come out soon. Nigga's gon' show their hand sooner than later."

"What's understood between us don't need to be explained. Once the sun shine down and reveal what the moon hid, the muthafucka gon' live the rest of their days in the dark. Keep ya head on the swivel at all times. Something is telling me we might have smoke today. There's plenty of us out here, but we can't be too laxed."

"No doubt." Fredo reached into a backpack and pulled out an earbud. "Here's the devices you told me to pick up. Communication is key. Everybody has one except Free because he ain't here yet. If something jump off, we'll be ready."

"My thoughts exactly. Don't give Free shit even if he shows up. The less he knows the better until I can prove he's involved or not. In the meantime, I'm going to treat his ass like a villain."

"Yo' gut has never been wrong, Cheno. Go with what it's telling you. I hope like hell them niggas don't come through here wreaking havoc because it's gon' end in mass destruction."

Fredo glanced around as the roar of approaching motorcycles approached the party. A slew of colors came closer and I noticed the body structure knowing tight away the riders were female. They all had on clothing which matched the color of their bikes and helmets.

"Who the fuck is that?" he asked.

A smile spread wide across my face when I recognized the bike I purchased for Honey leading the way. The Suzuki Hayabusa was money green. I created the custom color personally myself and it complemented her well. My heart pattered in my chest because I was anxious about seeing Charlie in what seemed like forever.

"That's Honey and the rest of their crew," I beamed.

"Ohhhh, they shittin' on 'em!"

Breeze swerved out of line leading them to an empty spot that could accommodate all of their bikes. My sister's outfit matched her bike perfectly and she was dressed down better than my ass. The custom blue Jordans she rocked were cold and I needed to know where she copped them from.

When Charlie removed her helmet, everything around me became a blur. My focus was strictly on her. Pink was her favorite color and her ass was hugging the hell out of the shorts she wore. Her breast sat up in the pink halter she wore. The diamonds glistened from her belly ring drawing attention to her tight abs. The thing that stood out the most was the short platinum blonde hair she sported. Had I not pissed her off, I would've been mad because she cut her hair. Honestly, the new look was gorgeous on her.

"Honey got a man? Baby girl looking scrumptious over there," Fredo asked damn near drooling.

"Shid, I don't think so. Yo' high yella ass don't stand a chance. She like 'em dark."

"What that mean? I'll do black face to get with yo' cousin."

Fredo was dead serious and the shit was funny as hell because he was a fool. I didn't take my eyes off Charlie and I felt a way when she turned in my direction without making a move to come my way. I told Fredo I'd be right back and trekked toward my people. Nothing mattered more than Charlie so, I didn't notice Larisa until she stepped in front of me.

"I know you're not going to walk past me without showing some love."

"Love? I've never shown you shit on that level. What brought you to that conclusion? I'm lost."

"Stop playing with me, Cheno. There's no way you caressed my body the way you do so well without loving me." She smirked.

Larisa was delusional as hell. What I did was fucked the shit out of her without passion then planted my kids on her face and ass. I'd never laid up and cuddled nor pillow talked with her but that's what she considered love. Yeah okay. Larisa approaching me was the last thing I needed. I'd stay away from her at all costs since she showed her ass with Charlie. All her calls and texts went unanswered and I planned to keep it that way. Except here she was.

I stared down at Larisa before taking a step to move around her. She blocked me once again wrapping her arms around my neck and went in for a kiss. I tilted my head upward to avoid what she was trying to do and her lips brushed my chin. I mushed her on the forehead making her step away from me. In an instant, Larisa was snatched by the back of her hair. She yelped out in pain.

Charlie came out of nowhere beating her ass. I had to blink a couple of times because I didn't see that shit coming. Grabbing Charlie's left arm, she used her right to punch me in the side of the head. Her blow had a lot of power behind it so she was able to go right back in on Larisa.

"I told you I would catch your ass before you called yourself coming for me!" Charlie said with every punch she landed to Larisa's face.

The girl didn't stand a chance and fought back with all her might but she was no match for what Charlie had in store for her. Being slung around like a rag doll, Larisa landed on the ground with a thud. Charlie was bend over fucking her up.

"Touch her and I will beat yo' ass. That's a one-on-one fight. Ya girl should've kept her muthafuckin' threats to herself," I heard Breeze say behind me.

I wasn't worried about Breeze throwing down with whoever she checked because my sister didn't fight females. That would've been an automatic murder charge. Snatching Charlie away from Larisa by the waist, I was finally able to stop her from doing any more damage than she'd already done.

"This nigga had you mesmerized when you should've been watching your back. You gon' learn to pick yo' battles wisely. I'm the wrong bitch to threaten."

Charlie screamed over my shoulder as I walked in the opposite direction. She struggled to get down but I wasn't about to let her fight again. Charlie started hitting me in the top of my head and I kept moving until she headbutted me in the face. I had no choice except to let her go almost dropping her on the ground.

"You bold as fuck to touch me, Cheno! Of all people you know not to touch me when I'm fucking a bitch up!" she yelled in my face.

"What the fuck I look like standing back while my woman fighting like a wild animal?"

"Are you referring to me or that bitch, Cheno?"

"You, Charlie. I'm talking about you," I said staring her directly in the eye.

Shaking her head, "I'm not your woman! That shit is dead because you stuck your dick in that bitch! For a muthafucka who says she means nothing to you, she was damn sure all in your face and comfortable with putting her lips on you!" Charlie screamed drawing more attention than I wanted.

I was the type of nigga that always kept my homelife private. There were some shit folks outside didn't need to know about me. My relationship or lack thereof with Charlie was one of them. At the moment, Charlie didn't give a damn who was listening. She had something to say and she was going to get it out. "Come talk away from all these people. You got these nosy muthafuckas all in yo' mouth and shit."

"For what? Half of these bitches out here probably had your nut on their breaths before," Charlie snapped. "The niggas ain't no different because they look just as dumb as you when they saw me walking up to you and the bitch. This shit ain't no secret. I was the only one out of the loop about everything you do when not in my presence. I know now and I'm no longer in the dark. So, what you trying to hide?" Charlie backed away from with pure disgust on her face. "Stay the fuck away from me, Cheno. Stop calling my phone, don't text me how sorry you are, none of that shit! Trash is what you want, trash is what you can keep chasing. Go where you are wanted because I don't want nothing to do with you anymore. Fuck you and everything you stand for!"

Charlie turned on her heels and left me standing there looking stupid. Honey ran behind her. I don't know what she was saying but whatever it was didn't convince Charlie to stay. In fact, it seemed as if it put fire under her ass to leave faster. Honey placed her hand on Charlie's hand and was shrugged off. Charlie jumped on her bike and sped off. Larisa's voice forced me to give her my attention.

"I'm pressing charges! Look at my face, Cheno!" she said removing an ice filled ball of paper towel away from her face.

Charlie did a number on her. She fucked Larisa up but she brought that on herself when she wrote a check her ass couldn't cash. Larisa should've just kept her damn business to herself. It doesn't pay to throw things in another woman's face. The outcome could be very painful and she learned the hard way.

"That's on you. Go to the hospital, Larisa. You may need stitches for that cut under your eye. If you want to press charges, it's your choice. I'd prefer if you took this stack and act like this never happened though."

"Oh, no, nigga. your hoe going to jail! Tell her ass to enjoy her freedom because I'm about to nail her to the cross. Save that stack for her books. What she did was felony assault with a deadly weapon."

"What weapon?" I asked confused.

"She had brass knuckles on her hand! How else did she bust my face open?"

I didn't mean to laugh but I couldn't help myself. Charlie whooped her ass like Mike Tyson used to do his opponents back in the day. She better make sure to get her head examined because something was definitely knocked loose.

"You trippin'. She hit you with her fist. Nothing more, nothing less. Do what you gotta do, Larisa. If the police pick her up for this shit, she won't sit long. Believe that. The offer for the stack is still on the table for you."

I walked off because she was talking crazy and I wasn't in the mood for the bullshit anymore. Larisa called me all types of muthauckas until the music drowned out her rant. The liquor table was my destination. I had a personal bottle of Hennesy and I didn't waste any time popping the top. Sitting alone watching everyone get back into the party, Lil Mike walked over with a blunt.

"You look like you need this," he said holding it out to me. "Man, Charlie wild. She beat the hell out of ol' girl. She looks familiar, but I don't know where I've seen her at. It will come back to me at some point."

"You know Larisa?" I asked blowing smoke out my nose.

"I don't know her per se. I have seen her somewhere before though. Don't worry, fam I have never slept with her." Lil Mike chuckled taking he blunt from me. "Cheno, it's not my place to say anything but I'm gonna say it anyway. Make shit right with sis. Charlie has always been solid and don't deserve nothing but the best. She's more than enough, brah."

"You don't think I already know that?" I gritted. "Yo' young ass trying to school me on females is ludicrous, nigga.

Still wet behind the ears with the smell of Similac on yo' breath."

"Tell me I'm wrong and I'll shut up."

"I'm not telling you shit! Change the subject. As a matter of fact, get yo' ass away from me. I'd rather be alone."

Lil Mike stood to his feet and walked away then turned back to me. "Cheno don't sleep on what I said. You gon' be around this bitch crying when a "Mr. steal yo' girl" type of nigga stepped in and sweep sis off her feet."

I pulled my Glock and pointed it at him. "Nah, I'm not gon' cry. I'm gon' shoot his ass just like I'm about to do you if you don't get the fuck away from me."

"Alright, boss. If you need a shoulder hit me up on bud," Lil Mike laughed pointed to the earpiece in his ear.

I ignored him and sat back lighting another blunt as I surveyed my surroundings. Nothing was out of the ordinary and Larisa was no longer on the premises which was a relief for me. The situation with Tank and Cheese had me on pins and needles because I knew they was going to clapback for what I did to their homies. Not to mention I disrespected the fuck out of them in death. In the streets nobody was safe when revenge was on the horizon. I went after one of theirs and one of mine could be next. Retaliation was a muthafucka. They started it and I damn sure was going to finish it.

Breeze sat next to me taking a sip from a cup. Without asking I already knew it was filled with Crown Apple whiskey. That was her drink of choice. We were close as hell and my sister knew me just as I knew her. She was waiting for me to address the issue with Charlie. I didn't want to talk about it. After a moment, she broke the silence that was rather thick between us.

"Cheno, you not enjoying your event. It's so unlike you so, lets shoot the shit. We might as well get it out in the open and deal with it."

I bobbed my head to the music then took a long toke of my blunt. "I fucked up, sis. Larisa approached me. I was on my way to love on Charlie when she tried to kiss me. She's been calling but I curved her ass at every turn."

"Stay the fuck away from that bitch, Cheno. Something ain't right with her for real. She's trying too hard and the shit looks forced. She calculated her move before you even walked away from Fredo. While she was watching you, I was watching her. Soon as you heading in that direction, she said *watch this. I'm about to fuck up his shit* before walking away from her friends laughing like an evil hyena."

"My dick tends to make 'em go crazy," I sniggered trying to make light of the situation.

"The shit is far from funny. The bitch gives me snake vibes. Where the fuck she come from? I've never seen her around Sia before they came to the shop and I was with her damn near every day. She appeared out of thin air and I don't like that."

"I've only known Larisa for a month. She sucked me off a couple times and I only fucked her three times. She means nothing to me. Just like all the other females that don't stand a chance of being with me."

"Fuck all these dusty ass hoes! Every one of them on take mode. The realest bitch is Charlie. She has had yo' back through everything since the day you went and picked her up from Indiana. I truly believe if you didn't have a pot to piss in and a window to throw it out she would still ride with you. Hell, she gon' hold you down until you're able to get back on your feet. That's how deep her love for you is." Breeze took a blunt from the cross bag she had across her chest and lit fire to it. After taking a pull, she blew out the smoke licking her lips. Nodding at a female who spoke to her and kept it moving, Breeze turned back to me.

"You gotta stop following behind the stragglers, brah. There's no future with them and it's the reason you may have lost the best thing that has ever happened to you. In my opinion, Charlie should've been left yo' ass. This ain't yo' first rodeo, nigga. She's better than me because I wouldn't tolerate the disrespect you dished out at every turn. Your rep and pockets are what these hoes see in your ugly ass."

I sat silently laughing lowly as I listened to my sister chew my ass up. She was far from finished. Breeze was going to lay all my dirt out for me to see from her perspective and I couldn't do nothing but respect it. The shit that niggas didn't give a fuck about or just didn't allow to bother them, females paid close attention to.

"How do you think Charlie feel seeing a bitch post on social media about what they had going on with you?"

"I can't control what another muthafucka do, Breeze! That ain't on me."

"It is on you! If you gon' be with somebody, choose a muthafuckin' side. Stop making her feel like she was the only one. True enough you looked out and showed her you loved her, but that ain't shit when you entertaining the next bitch. You gave these hoes the ammunition to throw that shit in her face then you expect her to eat the disrespect! Nigga, please. Brother or not, you dead wrong and I'm gon' leave it at that. Now, you don't have to talk about it no more. I gave you something to think about."

Breeze got up and rejoined her crew. The rest of the day went without a hitch and the turnout was pretty good. Things started to wind down close to midnight. I gave order to the cleanup people, said my goodbyes then jumped on my bike to head home. I had a slight buzz from the alcohol I'd consumed but it didn't affect my ability to get home. I arrived safely and went directly to my bedroom. Falling back on my bed, I closed my eyes and all I saw was my baby Charlie.

I didn't even realize I'd fallen asleep until my phone vibrated in my pocket. When I took it out, the time read 3am. The person calling was Larisa. Ignoring the call, I groaned as I rolled out of the bed to go into the bathroom. My phone rang again and I repeated my action. Decline.

"The fuck this bitch want? I'm done with the bullshit," I mumbled as I relieved my bladder.

The phone vibrated on the counter as I washed my hands. No one else was reaching out to me at that time of the morning. Except Larisa's worrisome ass. I undressed then stepped into the shower. My body relaxed soon as the water hit the top of my head. Quickly washing, I got out and dried off then went back into my bedroom with my phone in hand. Opening the text thread, I read what Larisa had to say.

(773) 555-0024: I need that money you offered not to press charges on yo' woman. I don't want a stack. Make it two. If not, I'll be going inside the station to file a report.

(773) 555-0024: I see you think I'm joking. Don't play with me, Cheno.

This bitch had to be out of her muthafuckin' mind. She sent a photo of herself standing outside the police station. Larisa had a bandage under her eye which had turned completely black. She had what looked like a blood clot in the corner. Charlie put the paws on her. I didn't think Larisa's injuries were severe as it was. She wasn't going to die but it was going to take a minute for her to heal.

Me: Aye, do you know what time it is? I'm not coming out to give you shit. Don't go in that building, Larisa.

She responded back in an instant.

(773) 555-0024: I knew you didn't love that bitch! She going to jail and her supposed to be nigga don't give a fuck LOL. Oh well, go back to sleep. I have business to handle right quick.

Me: Where the fuck you at?

(773) 555-0024: At the police station off 71st and Cottage. I'll let you know what they say when I'm finished.

Me: Nah, I'm on my way. Stay right there. I should be there in about twenty minutes.

(773) 555-0024: You got fifteen.

Me: That's not enough time!

I deleted the last message because as far as Larisa knew, I lived on 79th and Damen. It was the location I took her when we got together. I bought the property for tricking off purposes. Charlie didn't even know about the spot.

Me: Bet. Give me time to get dressed and I'll be on my way.

I threw on some clothes and grabbed my phone and keys. Doubling back, I went into the closet and counted out a thousand dollars and secured the safe. Larisa thought she was about to strong arm me out of my bread. It wasn't happening. She better be lucky I'm willing to give her what I initially offered. If Charlie's freedom wasn't in jeopardy the bitch would still be throwing out threats. I'd already hurt Charlie enough. Seeing her locked up behind my bullshit was something I couldn't allow to happen.

As I sped on the empty expressway to the city, Larisa's texted played in my head. The thought of killing the bitch sounded way better than e letting her fuck me out of money. Giving her what she wanted was no longer on the table by the time I exited the expressway on 71st Street.

(773) 555-0024: Your time is almost up.

Instead of texting back I pushed the call icon and waited for her to answer. Soon as she did, the light changed.

"I just turned off 71st and State. Hold yo' muthafuckin' horses," I barked.

Larisa hung up on me and that made me want to kill her even more. Her disrespect was out of hand. I was pissed for even falling for her shit. Deep down I had a feeling she was bluffing about going to the pigs. The pit of my stomach was churning and I automatically checked the rearview mirror. Nothing was behind me and I relax a little bit and kept going east toward Cottage Grove.

Breaking as I approached the stop sign on Michigan Avenue, Larisa called my phone back. My first thought was to ignore it but I stopped and put the call on speaker. Easing into the intersection, Larisa said something that made my heart skip a beat.

"You about to die, nigga."

Before what she said could register, an old school Chevy hit the side of my whip. I was pushed into a light pole across the street. My head hit the window and dazed me. A nigga shot into the passenger window several times. My body felt like hot coals were thrown on me. I reached for the lever on the side and forced the seat all the way back. The sound of an empty clip was music to my ears as I faded in and out of consciousness.

"I called the police!" a female voice said in the distance. "I'm tired of this shit! When y'all going to start fighting again? That's all I hear is gunshots. Scary ass fuckers!"

"Fuck you, bitch!" the unknown nigga hollered. "You lucky I don't know where yo' nosy ass at because I'll shoot the fuck out of you, too! Mind yo' business!"

Sirens blared in the distance then the sound of an engine roaring, followed by tires burning down the street echoed loudly in my ears. It sounded as if I was under water drowning. I fought hard to stay alert long as I could but it seemed like I was losing the battle. The sirens were loud and my silent prayers were even louder. The back passenger door opened and my first thought was the nigga came back to finish me off.

"Hold on. The ambulance is almost here," the same female voice I heard going back and forth with the gunman cried. "Is there somebody I can call for you?"

"Get-Get-Get my phone. The code is..." I struggled to get those words out before I passed the fuck out.

"No. No. No! Stay with me! Don't you dare stop talking. What's the code?" she was slapping my face repeatedly.

"71157."

"71157. Okay, what's your name?"

"Cheno."

That was the last thing I said before everything went black and my heart stopped beating.

To Be Continued…

Lock Down Publications and Ca$h Presents
Assisted Publishing Packages

BASIC PACKAGE $499 Editing Cover Design Formatting	UPGRADED PACKAGE $800 Typing Editing Cover Design Formatting
ADVANCE PACKAGE $1,200 Typing Editing Cover Design Formatting Copyright registration Proofreading Upload book to Amazon	LDP SUPREME PACKAGE $1,500 Typing Editing Cover Design Formatting Copyright registration Proofreading Set up Amazon account Upload book to Amazon Advertise on LDP, Amazon and Facebook Page

***Other services available upon request.
Additional charges may apply

Lock Down Publications
P.O. Box 944
Stockbridge, GA 30281-9998
Phone: 470 303-9761

177

Submission Guideline

Submit the first three chapters of your completed manuscript to ldpsubmissions@gmail.com. In the subject line add **Your Book's Title**. The manuscript must be in a Word Doc file and sent as an attachment. Document should be in Times New Roman, double spaced, and in size 12 font. Also, provide your synopsis and full contact information. If sending multiple submissions, they must each be in a separate email.

Have a story but no way to send it electronically? You can still submit to LDP/Ca$h Presents. Send in the first three chapters, written or typed, of your completed manuscript to:

LDP: Submissions Dept
P.O. Box 944
Stockbridge, GA 30281-9998

DO NOT send original manuscript. Must be a duplicate.
Provide your synopsis and a cover letter containing your full contact information.

Thanks for considering LDP and Ca$h Presents.

NEW RELEASES

BLOODLINE OF A SAVAGE **BY PRINCE A. TAUHID**

THE MURDER QUEENS 4 **BY MICHAEL GALLON**

THE BUTTERFLY MAFIA **BY FUMIYA PAYNE**

KING KILLA 2 **BY VINCENT "VITTO" HOLLOWAY**

BABY, I'M WINTERTIME COLD 3 **BY MEESHA**

THESE VICIOUS STREETS **BY PRINCE A. TAUHID**

TIL DEATH 2 **BY ARYANNA**

CITY OF SMOKE 2 **BY MOLOTTI**

STEPPERS **BY KING RIO**

THE LANE **BY KEN-KEN SPENCE**

MONEY GAME 2 **BY SMOOVE DOLLA**

THE BLACK DIAMOND CARTEL **BY SAYNOMORE**

CRIME BOSS 2 **BY PLAYA RAY**

THUG OF SPADES **BY COREY ROBINSON**

LOVE IN THE TRENCHES 2 **BY COREY ROBINSON**

TIL DEATH 3 **BY ARYANNA**

THE BIRTH OF A GANGSTER 4 **BY DELMONT PLAYER**

PRODUCT OF THE STREETS **BY DEMOND "MONEY" ANDERSON**

Coming Soon from Lock Down Publications/Ca$h Presents

BLOOD OF A BOSS VI
SHADOWS OF THE GAME II
TRAP BASTARD II
By **Askari**

LOYAL TO THE GAME IV
By **T.J. & Jelissa**

TRUE SAVAGE VIII
MIDNIGHT CARTEL IV
DOPE BOY MAGIC IV
CITY OF KINGZ III
NIGHTMARE ON SILENT AVE II
THE PLUG OF LIL MEXICO II
CLASSIC CITY II
By **Chris Green**

BLAST FOR ME III
A SAVAGE DOPEBOY III
CUTTHROAT MAFIA III
DUFFLE BAG CARTEL VII
HEARTLESS GOON VI
By **Ghost**

A HUSTLER'S DECEIT III
KILL ZONE II
BAE BELONGS TO ME III
TIL DEATH II
By **Aryanna**

KING OF THE TRAP III
By **T.J. Edwards**

GORILLAZ IN THE BAY V
3X KRAZY III
STRAIGHT BEAST MODE III
By **De'Kari**

KINGPIN KILLAZ IV
STREET KINGS III
PAID IN BLOOD III
CARTEL KILLAZ IV
DOPE GODS III
By **Hood Rich**

SINS OF A HUSTLA II
By **ASAD**

YAYO V
BRED IN THE GAME 2
By **S. Allen**

THE STREETS WILL TALK II
By **Yolanda Moore**

SON OF A DOPE FIEND III
HEAVEN GOT A GHETTO III
SKI MASK MONEY III
By **Renta**

LOYALTY AIN'T PROMISED III
By **Keith Williams**

I'M NOTHING WITHOUT HIS LOVE II
SINS OF A THUG II
TO THE THUG I LOVED BEFORE II
IN A HUSTLER I TRUST II
By **Monet Dragun**

QUIET MONEY IV
EXTENDED CLIP III
THUG LIFE IV
By **Trai'Quan**

THE STREETS MADE ME IV
By **Larry D. Wright**

IF YOU CROSS ME ONCE III
ANGEL V
By **Anthony Fields**

THE STREETS WILL NEVER CLOSE IV
By **K'ajji**

HARD AND RUTHLESS III
KILLA KOUNTY IV
By **Khufu**

MONEY GAME III
By **Smoove Dolla**

MURDA WAS THE CASE III
Elijah R. Freeman

AN UNFORESEEN LOVE IV
BABY, I'M WINTERTIME COLD III
By **Meesha**

QUEEN OF THE ZOO III
By **Black Migo**

CONFESSIONS OF A JACKBOY III
By **Nicholas Lock**

JACK BOYS VS DOPE BOYS IV
A GANGSTA'S QUR'AN V
COKE GIRLZ II
COKE BOYS II
LIFE OF A SAVAGE V
CHI'RAQ GANGSTAS V
SOSA GANG III
BRONX SAVAGES II
BODYMORE KINGPINS II
By **Romell Tukes**

KING KILLA II
By **Vincent "Vitto" Holloway**

BETRAYAL OF A THUG III
By **Fre$h**

THE MURDER QUEENS III
By **Michael Gallon**

THE BIRTH OF A GANGSTER III
By **Delmont Player**

TREAL LOVE II
By **Le'Monica Jackson**

FOR THE LOVE OF BLOOD III
By **Jamel Mitchell**

RAN OFF ON DA PLUG II
By **Paper Boi Rari**

HOOD CONSIGLIERE III
By **Keese**

PRETTY GIRLS DO NASTY THINGS II
By **Nicole Goosby**

PROTÉGÉ OF A LEGEND III
LOVE IN THE TRENCHES II
By **Corey Robinson**

IT'S JUST ME AND YOU II
By **Ah'Million**

FOREVER GANGSTA III
By **Adrian Dulan**

GORILLAZ IN THE TRENCHES II
By **SayNoMore**

THE COCAINE PRINCESS VIII
By **King Rio**

CRIME BOSS II
By **Playa Ray**

LOYALTY IS EVERYTHING III
By **Molotti**

HERE TODAY GONE TOMORROW II
By **Fly Rock**

REAL G'S MOVE IN SILENCE II
By **Von Diesel**

GRIMEY WAYS IV
By **Ray Vinci**

Available Now

RESTRAINING ORDER I & II
By **CA$H & Coffee**

LOVE KNOWS NO BOUNDARIES I II & III
By **Coffee**

RAISED AS A GOON I, II, III & IV
BRED BY THE SLUMS I, II, III
BLAST FOR ME I & II
ROTTEN TO THE CORE I II III
A BRONX TALE I, II, III
DUFFLE BAG CARTEL I II III IV V VI
HEARTLESS GOON I II III IV V
A SAVAGE DOPEBOY I II
DRUG LORDS I II III
CUTTHROAT MAFIA I II
KING OF THE TRENCHES
By **Ghost**

LAY IT DOWN I & II
LAST OF A DYING BREED I II
BLOOD STAINS OF A SHOTTA I & II III
By **Jamaica**

LOYAL TO THE GAME I II III
LIFE OF SIN I, II III
By **TJ & Jelissa**

IF LOVING HIM IS WRONG…I & II
LOVE ME EVEN WHEN IT HURTS I II III
By **Jelissa**

A THUG'S STREET PRINCESS | MEESHA

BLOODY COMMAS I & II
SKI MASK CARTEL I, II & III
KING OF NEW YORK I II, III IV V
RISE TO POWER I II III
COKE KINGS I II III IV V
BORN HEARTLESS I II III IV
KING OF THE TRAP I II
By **T.J. Edwards**

WHEN THE STREETS CLAP BACK I & II III
THE HEART OF A SAVAGE I II III IV
MONEY MAFIA I II
LOYAL TO THE SOIL I II III
By **Jibril Williams**

A DISTINGUISHED THUG STOLE MY HEART I II &
III
LOVE SHOULDN'T HURT I II III IV
RENEGADE BOYS I II III IV
PAID IN KARMA I II III
SAVAGE STORMS I II III
AN UNFORESEEN LOVE I II III
BABY, I'M WINTERTIME COLD I II
By **Meesha**

A GANGSTER'S CODE I &, II III
A GANGSTER'S SYN I II III
THE SAVAGE LIFE I II III
CHAINED TO THE STREETS I II III
BLOOD ON THE MONEY I II III
A GANGSTA'S PAIN I II III
By **J-Blunt**

PUSH IT TO THE LIMIT
By **Bre' Hayes**

BLOOD OF A BOSS I, II, III, IV, V
SHADOWS OF THE GAME
TRAP BASTARD
By **Askari**

THE STREETS BLEED MURDER I, II & III
THE HEART OF A GANGSTA I II& III
By **Jerry Jackson**

CUM FOR ME I II III IV V VI VII VIII
An **LDP Erotica Collaboration**

BRIDE OF A HUSTLA I II & II
THE FETTI GIRLS I, II& III
CORRUPTED BY A GANGSTA I, II III, IV
BLINDED BY HIS LOVE
THE PRICE YOU PAY FOR LOVE I, II ,III
DOPE GIRL MAGIC I II III
By **Destiny Skai**

WHEN A GOOD GIRL GOES BAD
By **Adrienne**

A GANGSTER'S REVENGE I II III & IV
THE BOSS MAN'S DAUGHTERS I II III IV V
A SAVAGE LOVE I & II
BAE BELONGS TO ME I II
A HUSTLER'S DECEIT I, II, III
WHAT BAD BITCHES DO I, II, III
SOUL OF A MONSTER I II III
KILL ZONE
A DOPE BOY'S QUEEN I II III
TIL DEATH
By **Aryanna**

THE COST OF LOYALTY I II III
By Kweli

A KINGPIN'S AMBITION
A KINGPIN'S AMBITION **II**
I MURDER FOR THE DOUGH
By **Ambitious**

TRUE SAVAGE I II III IV V VI VII
DOPE BOY MAGIC I, II, III
MIDNIGHT CARTEL I II III
CITY OF KINGZ I II
NIGHTMARE ON SILENT AVE
THE PLUG OF LIL MEXICO II
CLASSIC CITY
By **Chris Green**

A DOPEBOY'S PRAYER
By **Eddie "Wolf" Lee**

THE KING CARTEL I, II & III
By **Frank Gresham**

THESE NIGGAS AIN'T LOYAL I, II & III
By **Nikki Tee**

GANGSTA SHYT I II &III
By **CATO**

THE ULTIMATE BETRAYAL
By **Phoenix**

BOSS'N UP I, II & III
By **Royal Nicole**

I LOVE YOU TO DEATH
By **Destiny J**

I RIDE FOR MY HITTA
I STILL RIDE FOR MY HITTA
By **Misty Holt**

LOVE & CHASIN' PAPER
By **Qay Crockett**

TO DIE IN VAIN
SINS OF A HUSTLA
By **ASAD**

BROOKLYN HUSTLAZ
By **Boogsy Morina**

BROOKLYN ON LOCK I & II
By **Sonovia**

GANGSTA CITY
By **Teddy Duke**

A DRUG KING AND HIS DIAMOND I & II III
A DOPEMAN'S RICHES
HER MAN, MINE'S TOO I, II
CASH MONEY HO'S
THE WIFEY I USED TO BE I II
PRETTY GIRLS DO NASTY THINGS
By Nicole Goosby

LIPSTICK KILLAH I, II, III
CRIME OF PASSION I II & III
FRIEND OR FOE I II III
By **Mimi**

TRAPHOUSE KING I II & III
KINGPIN KILLAZ I II III
STREET KINGS I II
PAID IN BLOOD I II
CARTEL KILLAZ I II III
DOPE GODS I II
By **Hood Rich**

STEADY MOBBN' I, II, III
THE STREETS STAINED MY SOUL I II III
By **Marcellus Allen**

WHO SHOT YA I, II, III
SON OF A DOPE FIEND I II
HEAVEN GOT A GHETTO I II
SKI MASK MONEY I II
By **Renta**

GORILLAZ IN THE BAY I II III IV
TEARS OF A GANGSTA I II
3X KRAZY I II
STRAIGHT BEAST MODE I II
By **DE'KARI**

TRIGGADALE I II III
MURDA WAS THE CASE I II
By **Elijah R. Freeman**

THE STREETS ARE CALLING
By **Duquie Wilson**

SLAUGHTER GANG I II III
RUTHLESS HEART I II III
By **Willie Slaughter**

GOD BLESS THE TRAPPERS I, II, III
THESE SCANDALOUS STREETS I, II, III
FEAR MY GANGSTA I, II, III IV, V
THESE STREETS DON'T LOVE NOBODY I, II
BURY ME A G I, II, III, IV, V
A GANGSTA'S EMPIRE I, II, III, IV
THE DOPEMAN'S BODYGAURD I II
THE REALEST KILLAZ I II III
THE LAST OF THE OGS I II III
By **Tranay Adams**

MARRIED TO A BOSS I II III
By **Destiny Skai & Chris Green**

KINGZ OF THE GAME I II III IV V VI VII
CRIME BOSS
By **Playa Ray**

FUK SHYT
By **Blakk Diamond**

DON'T F#CK WITH MY HEART I II
By **Linnea**

ADDICTED TO THE DRAMA I II III
IN THE ARM OF HIS BOSS II
By **Jamila**

YAYO I II III IV
A SHOOTER'S AMBITION I II
BRED IN THE GAME
By **S. Allen**

LOYALTY AIN'T PROMISED I II
By **Keith Williams**

TRAP GOD I II III
RICH $AVAGE I II III
MONEY IN THE GRAVE I II III
By **Martell Troublesome Bolden**

FOREVER GANGSTA I II
GLOCKS ON SATIN SHEETS I II
By **Adrian Dulan**

TOE TAGZ I II III IV
LEVELS TO THIS SHYT I II
IT'S JUST ME AND YOU
By **Ah'Million**

KINGPIN DREAMS I II III
RAN OFF ON DA PLUG
By **Paper Boi Rari**

CONFESSIONS OF A GANGSTA I II III IV
CONFESSIONS OF A JACKBOY I II
By **Nicholas Lock**

I'M NOTHING WITHOUT HIS LOVE
SINS OF A THUG
TO THE THUG I LOVED BEFORE
A GANGSTA SAVED XMAS
IN A HUSTLER I TRUST
By **Monet Dragun**

QUIET MONEY I II III
THUG LIFE I II III
EXTENDED CLIP I II
A GANGSTA'S PARADISE
By **Trai'Quan**

CAUGHT UP IN THE LIFE I II III
THE STREETS NEVER LET GO I II III
By **Robert Baptiste**

NEW TO THE GAME I II III
MONEY, MURDER & MEMORIES I II III
By **Malik D. Rice**

CREAM I II III
THE STREETS WILL TALK
By **Yolanda Moore**

LIFE OF A SAVAGE I II III IV
A GANGSTA'S QUR'AN I II III IV
MURDA SEASON I II III
GANGLAND CARTEL I II III
CHI'RAQ GANGSTAS I II III IV
KILLERS ON ELM STREET I II III
JACK BOYZ N DA BRONX I II III
A DOPEBOY'S DREAM I II III
JACK BOYS VS DOPE BOYS I II III
COKE GIRLZ
COKE BOYS
SOSA GANG I II
BRONX SAVAGES
BODYMORE KINGPINS
By **Romell Tukes**

THE STREETS MADE ME I II III
By **Larry D. Wright**

CONCRETE KILLA I II III
VICIOUS LOYALTY I II III
By **Kingpen**

THE ULTIMATE SACRIFICE I, II, III, IV, V, VI
KHADIFI
IF YOU CROSS ME ONCE I II
ANGEL I II III IV
IN THE BLINK OF AN EYE
By **Anthony Fields**

THE LIFE OF A HOOD STAR
By **Ca$h & Rashia Wilson**

THE STREETS WILL NEVER CLOSE I II III
By **K'ajji**

NIGHTMARES OF A HUSTLA I II III
By **King Dream**

HARD AND RUTHLESS I II
MOB TOWN 251
THE BILLIONAIRE BENTLEYS I II III
REAL G'S MOVE IN SILENCE
By **Von Diesel**

GHOST MOB
By **Stilloan Robinson**

MOB TIES I II III IV V VI
SOUL OF A HUSTLER, HEART OF A KILLER I II
GORILLAZ IN THE TRENCHES
By **SayNoMore**

BODYMORE MURDERLAND I II III
THE BIRTH OF A GANGSTER I II
By **Delmont Player**

FOR THE LOVE OF A BOSS
By **C. D. Blue**

KILLA KOUNTY I II III IV
By Khufu

MOBBED UP I II III IV
THE BRICK MAN I II III IV V
THE COCAINE PRINCESS I II III IV V VI VII
By **King Rio**

MONEY GAME I II
By **Smoove Dolla**

A GANGSTA'S KARMA I II III
By **FLAME**

KING OF THE TRENCHES I II III
By **GHOST & TRANAY ADAMS**

QUEEN OF THE ZOO I II
By **Black Migo**

GRIMEY WAYS I II III
By **Ray Vinci**

XMAS WITH AN ATL SHOOTER
By **Ca$h & Destiny Skai**

KING KILLA
By **Vincent "Vitto" Holloway**

BETRAYAL OF A THUG I II
By **Fre$h**

A THUG'S STREET PRINCESS | MEESHA

THE MURDER QUEENS I II
By **Michael Gallon**

TREAL LOVE
By **Le'Monica Jackson**

FOR THE LOVE OF BLOOD I II
By **Jamel Mitchell**

HOOD CONSIGLIERE I II
By **Keese**

PROTÉGÉ OF A LEGEND I II
LOVE IN THE TRENCHES
By **Corey Robinson**

BORN IN THE GRAVE I II III
By **Self Made Tay**

MOAN IN MY MOUTH
By **XTASY**

TORN BETWEEN A GANGSTER AND A
GENTLEMAN
By **J-BLUNT & Miss Kim**

LOYALTY IS EVERYTHING I II
By **Molotti**

HERE TODAY GONE TOMORROW
By **Fly Rock**

PILLOW PRINCESS
By **S. Hawkins**

SANCTIFIED AND HORNY
by **XTASY**

THE PLUG OF LIL MEXICO 2
by **CHRIS GREEN**

THE BLACK DIAMOND CARTEL
by **SAYNOMORE**

THE BIRTH OF A GANGSTER 3
by **DELMONT PLAYER**

BOOKS BY LDP'S CEO, CA$H

TRUST IN NO MAN
TRUST IN NO MAN 2
TRUST IN NO MAN 3
BONDED BY BLOOD
SHORTY GOT A THUG
THUGS CRY
THUGS CRY 2
THUGS CRY 3
TRUST NO BITCH
TRUST NO BITCH 2
TRUST NO BITCH 3
TIL MY CASKET DROPS
RESTRAINING ORDER
RESTRAINING ORDER 2
IN LOVE WITH A CONVICT
LIFE OF A HOOD STAR
XMAS WITH AN ATL SHOOTER

www.ingramcontent.com/pod-product-compliance
Lightning Source LLC
Chambersburg PA
CBHW070509260626
47161CB00004B/1499